... "Suit your purposes?" The sound of a chair scraped wood, followed by its topple on hard wood. Leastways, that's how it sounded. Essie flinched at Alessandro's fury. He'd kept his passionate nature well hidden.

The Conte's tone hardened. "Sí. You shall betroth yourself and soon. 'Tis your duty. Just an heir or two. If Lady Kendra does not appeal, perhaps Lady Esmeralda is more to your tastes?"

The hair at Essie's nape raised, along with chilled pricks over her skin, air constricted in her throat. Her eyes began their awkward fluttered fury. Dust stirred in the room, and the furniture coverings billowed in protest. She fought an imminent sneeze at the stirring dirt.

"Lady Esmeralda? You have truly lost your faculties if your ambitions go so far as to bind me for life to a woman whose eyes flutter so furiously 'tis enough to create an avalanche in these Pyrenees Mountains?" Alessandro sniffed in disgust.

The Surprising Enchantress – book iii

Kathy L Wheeler writing as Kae Elle Wheeler

Acknowledgements

I have a very interesting friend who has been instrumental in helping me throughout this series with the French. Yes, (*oui*), it's true. I fail miserably at speaking French. She, however, has assisted me every step of the way. My sincerest thanks Linda Despieau.

My critique partners have also stepped up, batted me over the head: Christy Gronlund, Alice Clary, and Amanda McCabe. I would also add my thanks to Cheryl Pierson, Al Serradell and Margie Aston for their editing expertise.

This was a fun series to write, learn through. I will be moving on to other projects now, and will most likely find myself lost and floundering—but not for long, I hope.

Prologue

"WHAT ON EARTH ARE we to do about Esmeralda, Faustine?" Queen Thomasine, Maman to Prince Charming of Chalmers Kingdom, held out a freshly poured cup of tea for her twin, Cinderella's infamous Fairy Godmother. "Two of our girls are now married and settled, but I feel we have failed poor Esmeralda. And I fear her chances become slimmer each passing the day with her ill-fated...ahem...*eye affliction.*" Her last words ended on a loud whisper. "And I cannot quell the apprehension of Lady Roche's beneign behavior. She has been much too quiet of late. She is planning something, I fear."

Faustine accepted the steaming brew from Thomasine and blew a cooling breath over the rising steam. She braved a sip, choosing not to answer. She did not wish to talk of Esmeralda or the girls' buffoon of a mother. There was plenty of time to marry off the silly chit. Faustine had more important issues on her mind.

She studied Thomasine's elegant coiffure. Gray streaks displayed an age that mirrored Faustine's own. She drew in the fragrant oolong tea before finally answering Thomasine. "Did you have a particular suitor in mind, *ma chère*? She is a lovely young woman with her brilliant green eyes. And her hair is not *so* red as to deter any one eligible prospect. Perhaps she just hasn't met her true love yet."

An indelicate snort sounded from Thomasine. "Is there nothing you can do to help the girl with her unfortunate eye-batting?"

"*Non.* 'Tis something she, in time, must learn to control," Faustine said absently. "You shall see." She pressed her lips together. "My concerns regard her sister, Pricilla, my only son's wife."

"This is an old argument, Faustine. You shouldn't fret so. Your son and his bride are still youthful. There is plenty of time for grandchildren. Why the girl is but three and twenty at most."

"How much longer am I to wait, I ask?" Bitterness won through. "You could not possibly understand my frustration. After all, Edric is almost five and Arabella, three."

"Tsk, tsk, Faustine. You know that I am most willing to share my grandchildren with you. As I said, 'twill happen in time. And they are happy, *non*?" Mischievous mirth twinkled in Thomasine's eyes, furthering Faustine's irritation.

"*Oui, oui,*" Faustine threw out a hand, fingers brushing the air. "I suppose 'tis quite ungrateful for me to ask for more than my son's happiness." She gasped as a terrifying thought occurred to her. "You...you don't think she...Pricilla...is...is unable..." Life or death, Faustine could not complete the heinous thought aloud.

"'Tis a possibility, of course," Thomasine agreed. "But I feel inclined to point out the problem may not lay with your son's wife."

Faustine gaped. "*Mon...Dieu!* Bite your tongue!" She set down her cup lest the entire contents spill in her lap. "Do not dare to suggest such a thing. I would rather contemplate poor Esmeralda's eye-fluttering than consider such an unseemly topic." Faustine shivered at the mere thought of such a catastrophe.

"I agree, Darling. With my dear husband's passing and our mourning having ended, there is much on which to concentrate." Thomasine brushed away a stray tear, squeezing Faustine's heart.

"Preparations for the Coronation Ceremony are well under way. We've not much time as it is."

"I suppose you are right. But, honestly, Thomasine, no child in five years?" A shudder racked Faustine's body. She clasped her silver wand much like a child's security blanket. The ill-repaired apparatus Cinderella had stepped on and broken several years prior threatened to give way completely under the assault. Faustine forced her grip to loosen but squeezed her eyes shut in a silent appeal.

Thomasine was right. Concentrating on Esmeralda's unfortunate eye-affliction might help distract her from dwelling on Thomasine's unfortunate choice of words. Prophetic words Faustine prayed would not prove true.

Chapter 1

"YOU KNOW NOT OF what you speak. You are an insolent son," Conte Marcus Pasquale de Lecce bit out.

"Then perhaps you should enlighten me, sir." Visconte Alessandro de Lecce watched his father pace the near bare chamber like a caged lion. Aless knew he and the Conte resembled one another greatly in the set of their eyes and the harsh angle of cheekbones. But the past few years had aged his father at an alarming rate, shown by his thinning hair and the deeply creased lines etched in his forehead. A constant worry seemed to have settled over his father of late.

Aless snuck a glance at his timepiece for the third time. For three-quarters of an hour he'd been at odds with his father in a deserted wing of Chalmers castle. A strange location his father had requested for an interview and Aless was starting to fret for his father's mental faculties.

The Conte stopped, contemplating him for a long moment, mouth agape as though he might speak. But no, Papa clamped it shut and resumed his pace. Aless rubbed his temples to stave off an aching head. *Dio!* The man treated him as though he were the same age as Prince Charming and Princess Cinderella's young heir.

Without warning, the Conte stopped again. The abrupt stance raised the hair on Aless's nape. Wary, he watched, knowing things with his father rarely dispelled so easily. "Sit," his father commanded.

Foreboding trickled through him. Alessandro obliged, moving to an opulent, though faded, wing-backed chair, and slowly lowered his large frame. He stifled a sneeze for all the dust he'd disturbed.

The Conte stood before him, broad hands twisting. "I am not quite sure how to tell you this."

"Mayhap you should just say, save all the dramatics." Aless drummed his fingers on the arm of the chair impatient for the interview's conclusion.

"We are *Spagnolo*."

"*Sí*, on *Madre's* side. 'Tis no secret we are of Spanish descent." A sense of relief assailed him, and he shot his father an amused glance. But the Conte did not respond in return, instead compressing his lips firmly together walking the length of the room. Alessandro let out a sigh. "What is it, *Padre*?

"'Tis long past time you did your duty and married. Nobility, *Royalty*. We've a duty to our heritage." He flung out a broad hand. "We must begin building our legacy. The plans are almost in place."

Alessandro narrowed his eyes on the Conte. "Plans? Nobility? We are here for Prince Charming's coronation as king. What are you up to?"

"EDRIC, MY LITTLE PRINCE, we are missing out on family time. You know your Maman will be wondering where we have disappeared," Esmeralda chided her little charge. Edric was a gale of energy. A mass of dark curls and eyes were a perfect match of Cinde's rich browns and his Papa's outrageous charm.

The little progeny already had the aptitude for turning the saddest eyes on even the least gullible victim, charming them silly. His Auntie Cill came to mind as the toughest critic. Essie had seen the little thespian in action. Quite impressive he was, not to mention entertaining to observe, winding Cill round his chubby, pinky finger. Of Esmeralda's two sisters,

Cinderella and Pricilla, Pricilla was, by far, the more difficult to succumb to such tactics.

"Aunt Sessie, I would pray hide an' seek, *s'il vous plaît*," Edric begged.

"The word is 'play,' Edric, and we are late. We must hurry if we are to visit with the family before you and Bella are banished to the nursery for the evening." Essie kept her voice firm. One must maintain an image of control, regardless of the reality.

However, Edric was a master, evidenced when his fuller bottom lip poked out in petulance. He gulped to scream certain displeasure with his Aunt Sessie's unyielding words.

But Essie was not one of Edric's victims like his Aunt Cill, and verified her deftness. "Edric, I suggest you quell the impulse. Young princes do not bellow their tendencies to screaming, most especially, one of *your* maturity," she informed him blandly. Hands clasped before her, she presented a model of patience. *That* was imperative.

Edric stopped, seeming to consider her words. But when he handed her a brilliant smile she realized it was too late to rethink her stratagem. "I hide, Aunt Sessie, you *seek*."

The cheeky urchin whipped round and darted down a dimly lit corridor before she could blink.

"Edric," Essie called after him, stomping her foot. "Don't you dare!" But the ball of force had already disappeared. Essie lifted her skirts and bolted after him. The softly lit sconces intensified the depth of shadows as most of the chambers down this wing were dark and deserted. She poked her head through the first open door. "Edric, come out, *s'il vous plaît*," she called softly. How did one handle a misbehaving heir? Oh, she would blast the little scamp.

8

Silence.

Essie continued down the hallway. "Edric?" She angled her head, listening for the slightest sound. No Edric, only the murmurings of muted Italian—heated Italian. It sounded as if Alessandro de Lecce and his father were in a stormy row. She had an embarrassing ardor for the Conte de Lecce's elder son, Alessandro. They first made their appearance several years prior when Prince Charming was looking for his "mysterious princess."

With Alessandro de Lecce's dark hair and eyes, strong jaw and immaculate manners, Essie found him irresistible, though she'd noticed a certain broodiness about him of late that hadn't been apparent in previous years. He certainly couldn't have been involved with the Prussian—Austrian Wars. They'd ended ages ago. Of course, she'd never understood matters of war. She shook her head. No time to worry over that right now. She had to find Edric.

Besides, her little blinking problem hadn't abated in the least. Like the time Prince Charming's shoe slipped onto her own dainty foot, quite unexpectedly. She found herself betrothed to the future king. Why, the dust storm in her nervous state rivaled that of the Far Eastern desserts.

Something in the de Lecces tones drew her attention, and she inched forward. Why they would be in such a deserted portion of the castle was beyond her. She pulled up, shaking her head, then quickened her step. 'Twould not do to be discovered eavesdropping. Still, if the little monster did not show soon she would likely be forced to seek their assistance. She grimaced.

Wouldn't that be just her luck for the *Visconte* Alessandro de Lecce to witness—her incompetence of handling a rambunctious four-year-old. Her nerves simply could not take it. She was wont to send the Conte's elder son sprawling to land on his nicely shaped arse when her uncontrollable eye-batting kicked up at the stress of just imagining such a plight.

Essie blinked back a sudden sting of tears. Maman was right. She was completely unmarriageable with this idiotic affliction. And to someone of Alessandro de Lecce's pedigree, she was all but doomed to a court-appointed husband. Aggravated at the turn of her already obsessive insecurities, she shoved them away, knowing such introspection would only fester. She had a larger problem looming at the moment.

Essie paused at the next chamber, irritation escalating with each step. *Mon...Dieu*, nothing. Jaw clenched, she decided Prince Edric needed to be curbed with a demon. And she was the only one at hand. In a tone that would have served her well had she'd chosen to trod the boards she sang-song, "Humph, I suppose our little prince has made his way back, leaving me to find my way all alone." She ended on a dramatic sigh and a silent promise to blast the little imp.

Just as Essie ducked her way out, the first muffled giggle touched her ears. "Alas, 'tis a long trek," she said.

Silence. She scuffed her soft-soled shoes on the floor, pretending to walk away.

"I'm here, Aunt Sessie," Edric called.

She sighed. It was difficult to be angry with that tiny, high voice. "Where?"

"You must find me—'member? I hide and you seek." He giggled again.

Essie located a taper near the door and slipped back into the hallway to light it from a wall sconce. Lifting the candle overhead, she found herself in an old drawing room with sparse furnishings. Draped cloths and thickly layered dust covered every exposed surface. She moved deeper into the room and skirted several massive pieces before she spotted Edric's highly polished black shoe, poking beneath a white sheet over a settee. 'Twas practically a beacon.

She leaned down to grasp Edric's foot when Alessandro's words bounded down the hall so loudly they should have served as warning to pirates as far as the Mediterranean Sea.

"What are you talking about Nobility, Royalty, *Marriage*?" Alessandro sounded...furious.

"*Sì*. I vow Lady Kendra Frazier is perfect for you." Essie's stomach dropped and she could practically envision the Conte rubbing his hands together, warming to the topic.

The signs of panic started at the tips of her toes, working their way up through her blood stream. Her knees shook, soon followed by a tingling sensation in her fingers. The Conte was trying to marry off Alessandro to that nitwit, Kendra Frazier? Why, she was naught but a prissy—

"I shall not marry Lady Kendra, *Padre*," Alessandro said quietly.

Essie let out a held breath. It echoed in the chamber. Premonition angst rippled through her though along with the strongest wish to cover her ears. Yet, she was frozen in that bizarre world of morbid curiosity.

"No?" The Conte sounded amused now.

Obviously, Alessandro's steely resolve failed to penetrate.

Essie gripped the edge of the sheeted settee, relieved at the resolve she heard in Alessandro's tone.

"Why not? Lady Kendra suits my purposes adequately enough. Her *padre* as Earl of Macclesfield is a distant cousin to England's throne." The Conte's excitement permeated the air.

"Suits *your* purposes?" Chair scraped wood, then toppled on hard wood. Leastways, that's how it sounded. Essie flinched at Alessandro's fury. He'd kept his passionate nature well hidden.

The Conte's tone hardened. "*Si.* You shall betroth yourself and soon. 'Tis your duty. Just an heir or two. If Lady Kendra does not appeal, perhaps Lady Esmeralda is more to your tastes?"

The hair at Essie's nape raised, along with chilled pricks over her skin, air constricted in her throat. Her eyes began their awkward fluttered fury. Dust stirred in the room, and the furniture coverings billowed in protest. She fought an imminent sneeze at the stirring dirt.

"*Lady Esmeralda?* You have truly lost your faculties if your ambitions go so far as to bind me for life to a woman whose eyes flutter so furiously 'tis enough to create an avalanche in these Pyrenees Mountains?" Alessandro sniffed in disgust.

Essie froze as the insult struck; as surely as if his palm had landed across her cheek. She gripped her stomach at a sharp stabbing pain.

But apparently Alessandro de Lecce had not quite completed his annihilation—compelled to pound that final nail. "I have availed myself for your purposes long enough." His strong voice resonated harshly through the empty corridors. "Once this coronation ceremony is over, 'twill be time for us to return to our beloved Italy. I will not marry a woman able to change the weather on a whim. Not for you. Not for *anyone.*"

That voice, distinct, accented, belonging to none other than a man she'd pined over for five long years, gone, in the thrust of a knife straight through her lower abdomen—so great, she bent at the waist, gasping for air. The candle she held tilted in her trembling fingers, spilling wax on the dusty coverlet.

Tears spilled down her cheeks in a silent river of humiliation. Could a person expire from utter mortification? All those years, wasted in a silent vigil of love, praying he'd notice her—only to realize he'd most certainly noticed. *Mon...Dieu! Mayhap the floor could floor just open, s'il vous plaît?*

Essie sucked in deep, measured breaths, and stood. She dashed the tears away with her free hand lest Edric spy them. He would only further her embarrassment as a child was wont to do. All with innocent musings that would cut straight to her heart, sparing nothing, if he witnessed his favorite aunt sobbing like his three-year-old sister, not to mention his worry. He truly did love her, despite his mischievous pranks. And she must grasp her composure.

Determined footsteps echoed across the wooden floors. She was so lost in shock she failed to extinguish the flamed taper she held. She stilled as one of the marble statues in the ponds, Medusa, hopefully. Alas, to no avail. *Visconte* Alessandro de Lecce appeared in the chamber door, blocking her only exit. If only she could turn that...that scoundrel into stone!

Non, such was her luck. Her mortification was truly complete.

Chapter 2

FURIOUS, ALESSANDRO SOUGHT DISTANCE from his crazed sire. Drawn by the flame of a flickering candle, he perched in the arch of an open chamber to see the horrified expression of Lady Esmeralda. Her eyes glittered like the sharpest cut emeralds. Surely, 'twas the candle she held that had her eyes so green, sparking fire.

Had she overheard? He winced, realizing she could not have missed his over-zealous comments. His exact words reverberated so soundly through his head, 'twas a wonder they did not bound off the corridor walls. *I will not marry a woman able to change the weather on a whim.* Could this day get any worse?

The traces of tears were evidence enough. Aless swallowed a groan. Perfect. He was not in the habit of slandering young women, no matter how much he might fight marrying one. And slandering this one in particular left a sharp pain in his chest.

"*Signorina*? What are you doing down this deserted wing, pray tell?" Now that he thought on it, 'twas very odd. Had she followed him? *Dio!* That would be just like the Conte to manipulate such a situation. 'Twas no contest the chit faced issues securing a troth with such an off-putting flaw. He narrowed his eyes on her, but she drew herself up, back as straight as a steel bar. A cloak of...fury...rippled over the darkened chamber.

"Pray, do not trouble yourself, *Signore*," she said coolly, calmly. Her eyes remained unwavering, piercing him with daggers. Quite unnerving. She seemed almost...removed. Deafening silence filled the air. And then he heard it...a childish twitter.

Aless stepped forward. She stepped back, her message clear. But there it was again, definitely a child's muffled laugh. "What—or who, shall I say— are you hiding, *Signorina*?"

Suddenly, he was thanking the heavens her eyes only *fluttered* uncontrollably, rather than fire musket balls. He would have fallen to his death on the spot, mortally wounded, otherwise. Yet, they were not fluttering now. They glinted like etched crystal.

The child's laugh grew louder. Aless made his way toward the flame she held, toward glittering green eyes he'd ne'er notice before. *Only in his dreams.* Aless shook the unnerving thought from his head. Lady Esmeralda held her ground as turbulent fire emanated from her. He rounded what he supposed was a draped settee. The flame of the taper she held never once wavering.

The giggles, though muffled, could not be contained. Aless stood inches from Lady Esmeralda now. Soft-scented lavender wafted in a subtle wave across his senses. He leaned in. Had it really been four years since he'd smelled that enticing scent? Her eyes were quite striking in their brilliance. 'Twas amazing when one found oneself plummeting in their depths.

Hypnotic.

"Sir!" she barked. He started and stepped back. He shook his head, deciding he was out of his mind. Madness obviously passed through his bloodlines by way of the Conte.

Aless forced his gaze down where he saw the unmistakable shape of a tiny black shoe. He leaned over and lifted the edge of the sheet. Laughter burst from the small prince who crouched beneath.

"Aunt Sessie could not find me, sir." Prince Edric covered his mouth with a small hand. "She is but a girl."

Aless slid a slow gaze up the statuesque figure that comprised the young prince's Aunt Sessie. Taut shoulders, creamy bosom, compressed lips and angry sparks that threatened nothing short of death.

"*Sí*," he agreed softly. "She is but a girl."

HIS WORDS JERKED ESSIE into action.

"That is quite enough," she said to Edric sharply. "'Tis time to go." With forced effort she suppressed the fury in her tone. Edric must have read it, however, and stood quickly and grasped her hand.

"I was only praying," he told her contritely.

"Playing," she corrected sharply. "But we have wasted enough time." Her eyes never wavered from Alessandro. Anger was a comforting emotion, and she cloaked herself with it. Even with the dark simmering fire she sensed beneath the surface of Alessandro's sure facade, she took in the black hair held at his nape with a velvet queue, marveled at how she could still find him so attractive. 'Twould pass, she decided. He'd handed her the talisman to break free of her idiotic ardor. Though his looming figure, complete with broadened shoulders were of no help. She quashed any empathy at the embarrassed quirk of his well formed lips. It served him right. She knew neither one of them would ever speak of the matter henceforth. And that was fine with her.

"Are you angry with me, Aunt Sessie?" Edric asked.

She marched her small charge to the door. "Of course I am. You should never have darted down a deserted wing." She pierced Alessandro with a scathing glance. "You never know what kind of vermin you are susceptible to and likely bitten by." At the door she blew out the flame, set her taper on a nearby table, and tugged Edric into the dimly lit corridor.

"I suppose I deserved that," Alessandro murmured from behind. His breath stirred her hair.

She ignored him, determined her vigil of love had quite evaporated. It was a comforting thought. She softened her tone. "Edric, you must promise me not to run off like that again, *s'il vous plaît*."

He studied her for a long moment. Then, in a sudden move, he twisted his tiny body and threw his small arms about her massive skirts, voice muffled. "*Mais oui,* I promise. *Pease,* do not be angry with me, Aunt Sessie. I love you."

The sudden stop had Alessandro stumbling into her from behind. He grabbed her arm to steady her. His touch burned, but to jerk away would only let on how deeply he'd affected her.

When he didn't relinquish his hold, Essie finally shook off his grip and snatched Edric up, hugging him tightly. Tears clogged her throat, and she squeezed her eyes tight to quell any spillage. "It's 'please'," she corrected on a whisper. "And I love you, as well. I only live to keep you safe, my little prince."

Chapter 3

DUSK SETTLED BEYOND THE family parlor's picturesque windows.

"Where is Esmeralda, *ma chère*?" Queen Thomasine asked her son's princess, Cinderella. Faustine noted Thomasine's fond smile with glum resolve. Her glance happened up to see her son, Arnald, watching her with an amused quirk to his lips. Faustine cleared her expression. 'Twould not do to let him see her frustration with his wife, Pricilla. He was much too protective of her. Thomasine's words on each one's fertility still rung in her ears.

"Edric demanded her company before supping. He is changing. They should be along soon," Cinderella said.

"Cill, take Arabella, *s'il vous plaît*, just for a moment?" Cinderella thrust her sleeping daughter into Pricilla's reluctant arms without waiting for consent. The child never stirred.

"But—" Pricilla started. A blond, wayward curl fell obscuring her features.

Faustine hid a grin, watching Cinderella ignore the coming protest as she walked across the room and whispered something to Prince. Cinderella bestowed Faustine with a mild smile over her shoulder. Princess Cinderella thought to entice Pricilla with the familiarity a sweet child could bring forth. Thank the heavens the three-year-old was a sound sleeper. 'Twas not a bad plan.

Faustine inclined her head slightly acknowledging Cinderella's silent message. But then caught sight of Pricilla's narrowed eyes. Donning an innocent expression, Faustine shifted her gazed about the room.

Prince and Cinderella stood before the massive windows looking out over the dusky sky. Drink in hand, Arnald stoked the fire while Lady Roche, the girls' robust maman, took up one half of a large floral settee. All were gathered for the family's usual time spent with the children before they were banished to the nursery for the evening. The only two missing were Edric and Esmeralda. Thomasine's required standing supper policy allowed few excuses. In fact, childbirth seemed one of the only reprieves.

Faustine sighed and swung her gaze back to her daughter-in-law. Too late—Pricilla stood before her. "She is adorable, *non*?" she said benignly. Faustine's voice trembled slightly, unsure of what to make of Pricilla's blank expression.

"*Mais oui*," Pricilla agreed pleasantly. The air of nonchalance was suspect; then with a quick and unexpected move, Pricilla dropped Arabella into her lap.

Faustine caught Cinderella's pained expression when the princess lifted her shoulder in a 'we-tried' shrug.

Faustine put her lips to Arabella's soft forehead, her cloud of dark hair tickling her nose. Freshly washed children smelled so nice. 'Twas obvious Pricilla had no inkling in what she was missing, she thought with disgust.

"What important dignitaries are we expecting for dinner, Maman?" Prince asked. The boy was oblivious to any undercurrents, she'd wager.

"Conte de Lecce and his sons, Alessandro and Niccòlo have arrived, along with the Marques and Marquesa Giron of Spain. The Earl of Macclesfield and his daughter, Lady Kendra. A lovely young woman, I must say. Several others are en route." Thomasine sighed. "'Tis inevitable."

"I vow, the Conte and his sons have spent more time in Chalmers than they have in their own country of late," Arnald muttered.

"That is not true, my love," Pricilla chided, who had sidled alongside him. Faustine watched her son drop a protective arm about her shoulders with a bittersweet pang. "We've had no company in many months."

A stilted silence followed her words, the implication of King's death, just over a year past, settled over the chamber. She gasped. "Oh...*Dieu. Je suis désolée.* I am so sorry."

"Don't be silly, dear," Thomasine said. "This is life, *non?* We must go on."

"I find the Conte to be of excellent company," Lady Roche announced ignoring Pricilla's ill-timed outburst. Her large jowls wriggled profusely. For having such a large frame, she sat quite straight and prim. How such an evil woman birthed two lovely daughters was beyond Faustine's comprehension.

Faustine's thoughts fell on the two young Italian men. Frankly, she did not mind the sons so much as their over the top *Papa.* The Conte was just too polite, even for polite society. She narrowed her eyes on Hilda, fingers itching to flick her wand. She supposed it a blessing her hands were full at the moment. Rash decisions never boded well.

Perhaps a match could be arranged between the Conte and Lady Roche. Shipping both to Italy might suit everyone's purposes. Faustine patted Arabella on the back, soothing herself more than the sleeping child.

Bah. No such luck.

Chapter 4

HOW PERFECTLY DEFLATING, ALESSANDRO winced. The scene before him shook him to his core. The undying apology he owed Lady Esmeralda would be a difficult feat if her closed expression was anything to go by. He could not be sure why he even cared, but he did. A matter of honor, he supposed.

An awkward silence ensued, and with no choice but to escort the lady and her young nephew to the Grand Hall, the silence grew more stilted with each step. Aless studied Lady Esmeralda from the corner of his eye. Her lovely copper locks, artfully arranged, framed a heart-shaped face. Sweet, really, if one could discount the eye-batting phenomena.

Prince Edric grasped slender delicate fingers, skipping alongside, separating them from Aless. The barrier in which she used the young prince did not escape him. She uttered not a single sound, those full lips pressed together, set for battle.

"Aunt Sessie, do not be angry, *s'il vous plaît*," the child begged, somewhat prettily. Aless had the inclination that said prince, more often than not, won his way with that maneuver.

But her silence was stubborn. A kindred spirit touched him. The least she could do was placate the tiny urchin.

Aless knew a moment of irritation and answered for her. "I am certain your Aunt...what did you call her?"

"Sessie."

"Your Aunt Sessie," he continued, "is not truly angry with *you*."

"She's not?"

"I *am* present, you know," his Aunt Sessie bit out. A sudden burst of humor spilled through Aless, knowing she'd practically choked voicing the words. Aless clamped down on the inside of his cheek to stifle the sudden urge to laugh. 'Twas a surprising thought, considering his slip of unwieldy criticism.

After an interminable trek, they stopped in the Grand Hall. Lady Esmeralda turned narrow eyes on him. "Thank you for your escort, *Signore*. I wish you an uneventful search for the perfect bride. No unwieldy breezes, as it were."

He cringed. Her timely spear was pointed and excruciatingly direct. His words had been inexcusable. And Aless found he had nothing to say, so he offered a sharp bow, and made a quick escape to the visitor's parlor to lick his wounds with a much needed pre-supper brandy. How awkward and demeaning to place himself in such a graceless quandary. Now he had much to make up for. 'Twould have been too easy to blame his father for such lack of comportment. But *no*, the words erupted from *his* mouth, not the Conte's. No matter where he wished to consign blame, it belonged squarely on his shoulders.

A strategically placed footman quickly opened the parlor's French doors for Aless to brush through. The room's understated elegance in cream was accented with subtle touches of rose, and did little to soothe his self ire. Neither did the cozy fire in the grate, even with its wafting warmth. Seeing the Conte near the hearth, brandy glass already in hand brought his words crashing over his head. His father's brooding expression was quickly replaced with the polished façade of eloquent patience upon Aless's entrance.

Niccòlo, Alessandro's younger brother, had stationed himself as far away as possible. The lucky cur had wisely taken refuge in the opposite corner. The Conte stalked to the shelf and poured a second glass and held it out to Aless, message plain. With no choice but to accept in gracious defeat, he made his way across the room.

"*Grazie, Padre,*" he said, taking the proffered glass. He tossed back the two fingers of liquid gold in one gulp. It burned going down, drawing a frown from the Conte. There was a measure of satisfaction in that. He moved to pour another.

Wiping his brow of disapproval, the Conte glanced round and demanded softly. "We shall meet tonight. At the pond."

"Which pond would that be, *Padre*?" A surprising quirk of humor touched Aless, this one of the more sardonic variety. His father's theatrics would not play out well with an audience, and Aless took advantage. He hid a grin behind another fortifying sip. "There are twelve Greek statues. Each one resides in its own pond."

"Impudence does not suit you," the Conte snapped. "Eros, will suffice, 'tis the closest one, yet situated beyond prying ears. After we sup. Do not be late."

Before Aless could issue a retort, the parlor doors swung wide where the earl of Macclesfield and his daughter, Lady Kendra Frazier, entered. She walked in on light, ethereal steps.

She was the epitome of an English lily with her petal soft skin as pale as milk, lovely pale blue eyes, and pale blond hair. She struck him as—pale.

Aless could detect no flash of fiery brilliant sparks from that faint blue gaze. It would be difficult to find fault in the deliberately twirled curls piled to perfection atop a feminine head held high on such slender shoulders. She certainly had breeding. *Dio!* He might as well be considering a horse.

From his place near the hearth, Aless watched the Conte saunter over to greet the Earl, any sign of prior irritation *or* madness, dissipated. His father, ever the suave Italian gentleman, bowed over Lady Kendra's gloved hand. She twittered prettily. *Padre* turned a raised brow in his direction. So subtle. The bite of sarcasm was not lost on him, even in his own head. The message hits its mark. Lady Kendra would do just as well as Lady Esmeralda. It made no difference whom he married so as long as he did.

Nobility.

Royalty.

Horses.

The Conte placed Lady Kendra's hand on his arm and turned toward Alessandro. He choked back a groan, plastering a smile on his face, and watched the Conte cover the distance between them. No one said an Italian Conte's son could be any less charming than *the* Prince Charming.

"Alessandro, may I present Lady Kendra." His father could not have been more obvious had he said the words aloud: *I give you Lady Kendra, take your pick of horse flesh.* Instilled etiquette demanded Aless click his heels and bow low over her extended gloved hand.

"Lady Kendra," he murmured.

Thankfully, a timely interruption of the royal family saved Aless from further exchange. The hum around the room faded quickly to an unnatural silence. Aless found his gaze riveted on Lady Esmeralda.

Something struck him as remarkably different since their earlier meeting—was it only an hour ago?

It took him a moment to realize that difference. Her eyes weren't batting furiously. In fact, a shimmer of iridescent glow seemed to surround her. Aless knew she'd harbored quiet feelings for him over the past few years and he'd worked diligently at not encouraging them by keeping a polite distance. Only on the battlefield had he allowed indulgences in thinking of her. But watching her now sucked the very breath from his lungs, stealing every faculty he possessed. Mayhap he was more ready to be shackled than he'd believed.

Realistically, knowing she'd heard his hurtful words should not trigger such a physical reaction. But for some unexplained reason she drew him like a moth to flame. Her eyes met his, bold and *steady,* and all but screamed a silent challenge. *Sí.* That pert chin lifted, those delicate shoulders squared. Every curve of her slender body spoke of a defiance she'd never before displayed. Perhaps he was seeing beyond the furious blinking that instead had him sinking into the depths of dark emeralds previously unnoticed. Should he decide to pursue this new Lady Esmeralda, the conquest would be a difficult one. One of his own making.

A familiar twinge of humor pinched his cheek and he shot her a conspiratorial wink. She flinched and heightened color dotted her cheeks. Where her eyes wuld have flickered neverously before, her chin lifted and she held her stance. Air seeped slowly into his lungs, and the iron band constricting his chest loosened.

Aless made his excuses to Lady Kendra and navigated his way around the room. Like a jungle cat, he stalked his prey. Lady Esmeralda had managed her way to large windows facing the night sky by the time he'd reached her. She appeared oblivious to the others, seeming to contemplate the twinkling stars.

Once more, soft lavender assaulted him as he sidled close. He drew in the subtle fragrance with a deep inhalation. The apology, he reminded himself.

"Lady Esmeralda," he said softly. He clicked his heels together and offered a short formal bow.

She stiffened slightly before turning to greet him with unflinching, accusing eyes. Protocol required her acknowledgement, and he was relieved she adhered. "*Signore.*" Subtle sarcasm was not lost. He deserved that, and worse.

"I wish to humbly apologize for my egregious remarks this afternoon. I am sure you overheard."

She graced him with a bland smile. "Remarks?" The toss of her head was slight but mutinous. "I have no notion of what you speak, *Signore.*" She started to edge away, her desire to escape, fervent. She should be so lucky. *Dio.* Two could play this game. He was a strategist by nature. War had taught him that, and he planned to win this battle.

"*Excusez-moi …*"

Ignoring her excuses, he grasped her hand and placed it on his arm, piercing her with suspicious, narrowed eyes. "No." He kept his tone mild and pleasant for the benefit of their surroundings.

"*No? Excusez-moi?* Did you just say…*no?*" Oh, but she was lovely when her temper was riled. She tried to snatch her hand away. The maneuver was unsuccessful as he maintained a firm grip. She was going nowhere. Her gaze remained steady, brilliant, controlled.

He was enthralled. "No," he reiterated, grinning outright.

Her lips tightened. "*D'accord, Monsieur*! I heard your comments," she hissed, then glanced about.

Heat crept up his neck as he followed her gaze. "No one can hear, *Signorina.*" Aless wished she would plant a fist in his face. And by the clenched fist at her side, he was certain she wished so as well. But she was far more gracious than he deserved.

Fury racked her petite frame. "How uncouth of you to address such an issue in polite company. 'Tis beyond...beyond..." She seemed to struggle to complete her thought, squeezing her eyes shut.

A blush flamed her cheeks—so engaging, he clenched his one open palm into a fist. His gaze dropped to her lush red lips, and he felt an overpowering urge to...to...*kiss* her.

She drew herself up to her full height, humorous in and of itself since she only reached his chin, and pulled in a breath. She let it out slowly before opening her eyes to meet his. "Apology accepted, *Signore*," she said, voice arctic, flat. Yet those eyes told a different story. Their fiery brilliance, glittering gems so compelling, that for a moment he lost sense of his purpose. "I believe I have suffered humiliation enough, *Signore*."

Aless shook his head in an effort to gather his wits. "I must atone—"

"Pray, do not concern yourself on my account, *Monsieur*." She'd shifted to a pitch so sweet his teeth ached, and said softly so as no one could overhear, "Do not think I am not aware of my shortcomings, Signore de Lecce."

His name from her lips did something to his heart, but with a suffering sigh, he said, "The shortcomings are my own, *Signorina*."

She was quick to agree. "*Certainement, Signore*. I have no argument with you on that score." She gave him another brilliant smile, putting him off his guard. His grip loosened. 'Twas a mistake, he realized too late, when she seized the opportunity to escape to her sisters. He watched thoughtfully, as she weaved her path.

Unclenching his hands, Aless flexed his fingers, allowing the blood to circulate. He had the perfect out through Lady Kendra. Why, then, did the thought not excite him as it should?

"Dinner is served."

Chapter 5

ALESSANDRO DREADED THE COMING meeting with the Conte. Out of respect, he knew he had no choice. The nip in the air was a refreshing change from the pompous dinner Aless had just suffered through. Seven courses. *Dio.* No one would starve under Charming's tutelage.

Though he'd known the family for—well, years, now—he still could not shake the feeling of Sir Arnald's despite the assistance he'd given in the man in saving his wife from those damned villains several years ago. 'Twas surely the luck of the gods, and the queen, that had him seated out of Arnald's direct line of sight this night. Prior to that, before the prince and the princess married, he suspected Arnald wielded odd powers.

The memory seared him like it was yesterday. Seated quietly at dinner that eve, one moment Aless had been holding his wine, the next found him wearing it. He considered Prince Charming's knighted cousin from a hooded gaze. The man's façade of innocence was just too *innocent.* He was massive, larger even than the prince. An intimidating figure, but Aless knew him better now.

The notion that Arlnald forced him to spill the wine on himself was nothing short of outrageous. Had Arnald compelled him into that disaster— *against his own will?*

Impossible. No one could *compel* another against their will. Aless shook his head and watched his father make his way down the terrace steps.

As the Conte winded his way toward him, Aless considered the shift in the movement of modern entertainment in London. Things were well on their way toward the phenomenon of mesmerism. Parties were springing up across the continent seeming quite the rage. But London was miles away, they were in the depths of the Pyrenees, he assured himself. He stifled a groan. His father's madness was surely becoming his own.

He, himself, had actually dabbled in the dark arts at one time. Child's play, of course—young men playing at growing up in their school days. Yet, he shivered again at the memory. Some of the illusions were quite popular, but others had them being accused of witchcraft, and more than once found him and his friends being chased from marketplace fairs. Even all in fun, a crowd could be quite unpredictable. It was then Aless decided to concentrate on his studies. Though his friend Joseph had not only dabbled, but became eerily proficient at the craft. Perhaps, Sir Arnald had studied mesmerism as well.

Aless drew in a cool breath and turned to meet his father's penetrating scrutiny. The Conte had chosen their meeting place well. Guests could observe the two of them speaking without fear of being overheard. Why that should matter sent a shudder rippling down Aless's spine? But suddenly he was very relieved at the understated privacy. "Why all the clandestine behavior, *Padre*?"

The Conte's expression took on a stubborn demeanor Alessandro had not seen since he was a child. "There is some...some..." He threw out a hand as the words seemed to escape him.

"What? Magic dust in the air?" He gave his father a patronizing smile, but the Conte too caught up in his theatrics, ignored it.

"*Sí.* That is it. Something—'tis not normal. I see a shimmer in the atmosphere. As if someone hovers above, listening. You do not sense it?"

"Don't be ridiculous," Alessandro said, not without impatience. He pushed a hand through his hair. To mention the twinge of bewitchment— *enchantment*, as it were—something he was certain he'd experienced a good four or five years before, seemed preposterous. Then again...and now, as the Conte spoke of *magic dust*...of all the nonsensical blather....enough was enough. "Shall we get to the matter at hand?" Aless snapped.

"*Sí, sí.*" The Conte clasped his hands at his lower back and paced before Alessandro, his mien serious. He scanned the area, then said in low tones, "We are *Spagnolo.*"

"Of course we are, from the side of your *madre.* We have established that." Aless shook his head, wondering what had come over his father. He scrubbed a palm over his face, praying for patience.

"You do not understand me, *no*?"

"Apparently not," he muttered under his breath.

"Your grandpapa, he was *spagnolo* as well. As was *my padre.*"

Frustrated, wishing he'd make his point, Aless retorted, "That's impossible. We are Italian. Italian nobility."

"*No,* we are of *spagnolo* nobility," he said, chin lifted. Dare Aless think it—maniacally? But his father had not finished. "We have been hiding in Italy since I was a young child."

Alessandro shook his head, letting out a slow breath. He was finding an elusive willingness to endure. "*Padre...* you are overwrought and need your rest," he said gently.

The Conte's obvious agitation had Alessandro surveying the grounds.

"You feel it too? The ears?" his father asked softly, hardly above a whisper.

The ears? "Just...continue, *per favore.*" Would they make it to their beloved homeland before Alessandro was forced to have the man committed? He was starting to worry for his father. They'd never been close, but Aless surely owed his father his loyalty. And, he supposed, 'twas true he should be thinking of an heir. As the elder son, he had a duty towards such. But so soon? A picture of brilliant green eyes floated through his mind. He shook away the image.

"Chalmers Kingdom belongs to *me*! Conte Marcus Pasquale de Lecce-Soliz." The Conte pounded his chest emphatically.

"What! *Padre,* do not speak so," Alessandro hissed. A sudden wind stirred the trees as if gasping his exact sentiments.

"Do not patronize me, my son, we shall have what rightly belongs to *us*...I vow it." The Conte resumed his pace before the pond. "You *will* marry! 'Tis time. Time to rebuild our empire," he commanded in a hushed tone. "Niccòlo as well. He is of all of two and twenty after all, and we have much work to accomplish in a short time."

Reluctant, horrified fascination filled Aless, watching the Conte rub his hands together. As if his father had just completed a particularly difficult task, as if matters now resided under their proper control.

Aless straightened and crossed his arms over his chest. "And when do you propose a wedding take place, hmm? The coronation ceremony is but a week hence. That might raise suspicion, *no*?"

The Conte stopped and considered Alessandro. Although tempted to look away from the intensity of his father's gaze, Alessandro knew that would be a vast mistake. The Conte began his tread once more. "Ah, *sí*. You make a valid point." He nodded.

Aless smiled; relieved his words were finally heard. "Of course, I do."

"I understand. She shall have to be ruined."

"*What!*"

"What? Oh, *no, no*. You misunderstand me. I am not saying there is a need to compromise her body. But..." his father leered at him. "...imagine the—"

"Stop! Don't say it." Groaning, Aless buried his head in his palms.

"*No*. There are other ways." The Conte threw out an impatient hand. "If you are caught alone with her—that is sufficient, *no*?"

"Who, *Padre*?" Rage filled Alessandro, and his tone turned dangerous in its calm. The Conte did not seem to pick up on the fact.

"Lady Kendra. Who did you think I meant?" With that little announcement, his father spun on a booted heel and made his way back to the terrace.

"You are quite mad, sir," Alessandro said softly, watching him march away.

Chapter 6

LADY KENDRA FRAZIER SLIPPED from the retiring room, hoping to catch a single glance of Alessandro de Lecce before Papa declared it too late for a young miss. She was all of eighteen years and he treated her as if she were still in the nursery. Why, she'd spent all of last season in the most exclusive of ballrooms dancing with earls, marquesses, and viscounts. And even one duke! Though he was squatty and old, she admitted wrinkling her nose. He'd smelled bad too.

She paused before the looking glass in the Grand Hall and smiled at her reflection. Good, every curl remained in perfect placement. She pinched her cheeks for tint, dug her straight and perfect teeth into her bottom lip for fullness and added color. Now, if only she could convince Papa that she was old enough to use lip paint. He would kill her first. Ten years ago she'd found rouge in her governess's possession. Papa's reaction was an apoplectic fit.

Kendra smoothed away the pout. It mattered not. She was by far the youngest and prettiest female in attendance. Lest, so far. She had no doubt she and Alessandro de Lecce would make the prettiest babies. A practiced curve touched her lips. All in all, he would do quite nicely. Soft steps sounded behind.

"Lady Kendra? Is all as it should be?"

She spun to the softly questioning tones of Princess Cinderella. The princess, outfitted in heavy dark blue velvet, was a picture to behold. She wore a delicate diamond tiara Kendra would have loved to own. Deep brown eyes, full of kindness, charmed Kendra into smiling back.

"Oh, yes, ma'am, *oui,* Your Ex...Excellency. I am expecting to have a wonderful adventure on my leave from England." Kendra marveled at the princess's dark hair and exotic eyes, surprised Prince Charming had chosen someone so different from her own pale beauty.

"As well you should," the princess smiled. "We've planned several outings to the various ponds during your visit. Each of the garden's ponds hosts a magnificent statue of a Greek god, you know."

Her conspiratorial tone engaged Kendra—made her feel as if she were truly welcome. No one at home even tried. 'Twas mostly ridicule and insinuations of her *stupidity*. "Greek gods?" Kendra adjusted her gloves.

"*Oui.*" The princess' rapture colored her features. A sudden insight of His Excellency's desire stunned Kendra. "Aphrodite, Eros, Hermes, Zeus."

"Oh, my," Kendra murmured. "You must be an avid reader." Kendra hated reading, with a passion.

"*Mais oui.* But seeing them, I'm certain you will be impressed. When I first arrived, I was absolutely enthralled. My sisters and I read stories to the children each morning on the different ones, just as my own *Papa* did. I bid your company to join us."

"R-r-read?" The sound emanating from Kendra hardly sounded her own, having jumped two octaves. Heat flooded her cheeks.

"*Oui.* We convene in the library at ten on the clock. Perhaps you'd care to join us." The princess hooked an arm through hers. "Now, come along. Surely we've been missed, my dear."

"Y-y...yes, ma'am." Panic choked Kendra. She could hardly decline reading with the royal family's children. With a steady, hopefully *concealed* breath, she reasoned that as long as they did not expect *her* to read she could surely manage to muddle through. "I...I'll be there. Thank you."

The thought absolutely nauseated her.

Chapter 7

THE NEXT DAY, EARLY morning sunlight streamed through the chamber where a hoard of seamstresses hard at work seemed oblivious to Essie and her sisters' ramblings. At least, Essie fervently hoped. She wandered over and glanced at the intricate embroidery on a rose colored gown of soft silk. Lilies in ivory, dotted with pearls, lined the bodice.

"Beautiful," Essie murmured.

"That's perfectly horrid, Essie," Cinde gasped. With raised arms, one seamstress fashioned mounds of the creamed silk around Cinde's slender body. "That is a dreadful area of the castle. You say the de Lecces were meeting in a deserted wing? Quarrelling?"

"*Oui*, horrid," Essie bit out, spinning back to her sisters. She could not bring herself to confess what she'd overheard. 'Twas too humiliating. But who could blame Alessandro, she thought glumly before glumness migrated to self-disgust. Would *she* choose to be bound to another whose eyes batted so furiously they could cause an avalanche?

Essie leaned forward and peered closely at Cinde's gown. She had to bite her tongue to keep Alessandro's damning words spilling from her lips. "My, these buttons are lovely," she murmured, pretending to seek a closer inspection of Cinde's coronation gown. "Hundreds of them. 'Twill take an army to dress you."

"I believe you are holding something from us," Cill accused her. The lack of conviction in her tone had Essie meeting Cinde's eyes from the looking glass in joint concern.

Essie abandoned her position near the seamstress and moved next to Cill. She touched the back of her hand against Cill's forehead. "You're pale but you do not feel warm to the touch."

"I'm tired," Cill snapped. "What did you really overhear?" She sunk down in a plush chair, eyes drifting close. "He said something you are not sharing. 'Tis all but written on your plainly-spoken face. You have been in love with the man for nigh on five years."

"Well, I vow I am not so any longer," she declared. "Edric ran down that darkened hallway against my explicit instructions. Alessandro was arguing with his father," she defended. "Loudly. They could be heard in the South Seas."

"Well, whatever you heard, it must not have been good." Cinde turned and grasped her hands. "You don't need him," Cinde told her. "There are much better men out there for you."

"I knew it," Cill said. Only her mouth moved.

Essie frowned at the lack of emotion coming from the most pragmatic, skeptical of her sisters. She watched Cill give Cinde a weak smile.

"One who wouldn't mind a nice sharp breeze in the dead of winter?" Essie said.

"There's always summer..." Cill quipped, rising.

"You know," Cinde started. "Mightn't there be a solution to your dilemma?" The question alone was enough to garner Essie's full attention.

"Cinde, do not promise more than you can deliver," Cill warned.

"Ignore her," Essie said. "I am all ears."

"There is a fairy godmother on the premises."

"Cinde," Cill implored. But thankfully, Cinde ignored her.

"*Oui*?"

Cinde shrugged her shoulders offhandedly. "Mayhap, she can help. 'Tis all I'm saying, I, of course, can promise nothing."

Cill groaned and strode to the windows and tried to unlatch it. "We don't know that that's possible," she said.

Essie watched her struggle, and after two unsuccessful attempts stalked over and pushed Cill gently aside and performed the task herself.

Cinde circled to face them, graceful skirts billowing in her wake. "Surely there are rules?"

Cill snorted before pushing her head through the open window. She drew in a deep breath of the cool morning air—air that had Essie shivering.

"'Tis a good question. How might we find out?" Essie was enthralled with this thread of conversation. "I must admit my unwavering interest if such a possibility exists. Alleviating this unbearable affliction would be heavenly."

Cill sighed. "Need you be so dramatic, Essie?"

"'Tis all well and good for you," she said bitterly. "You are not the one who comes under suspicion when the slightest gust of wind kicks up, regardless the time of year."

"There is that," Cill allowed. "But surely you don't believe there is a Fairy Godmother rule book? Why, the idea is preposterous. Besides, we don't even know who your fairy godmother is, Cinde. You've never said. Why is that, I wonder?"

Essie's hopes were dashed when Cinde frowned. "Well, to be honest, I...I don't know who *she* is. I suppose 'tis the floating shimmers in the atmosphere when she was about. But I'm certain she is beautiful and generous. I do know she wears a pink frothy gown." She tapped a finger against her chin. "I've heard tell of a magician who lives in a cottage near the sea. Chevalier Joseph Pinetti. Mayhap, he could answer a few *subtle* questions." Cinde said.

Essie's gaze moved to Cill who had turned from the window, a thoughtful crease in her brow.

Cill, the usual voice of reason, said, "it would have to be very subtle. 'Twould probably not do for the real fairy godmother to get wind of our machinations."

"*Oui*," Cinde agreed frowning. "That is so. She might decide to bestow a far worse curse."

"What could be worse than an eye affliction that can move mountains?" Essie said glumly.

Cill's lips twitched in the humorous irritating way Essie knew to be her smirking trademark. "Well, she could make your feet grow larger, *oui*?"

"The fairy godmother did not make your feet grow larger, Cill. They were already large!"

The insult hit its mark and Cill pressed her lips together. The fit of temper storming Cill's features was cut short.

"I shall be very happy when this coronation ceremony is over." Cinde frowned. "I seem to have little enough time for my children with all these fittings and such."

Cill stormed from her place at the window and grasped a startled Cinde by her upper arms. "In less than a sennight you shall be crowned queen, for the sake of heav'n. Perhaps you should have thought of that before marrying your beloved prince," Cill chastised.

After the initial shock of Cill's profound statement, Essie could not help her giggle as she watched realization sweep Cinde's features. Essie tried to muffle it with a fist, to no avail, which drew an unexpected burst of laughter from Cill.

Cinde swallowed soundly. "Oh," she squeaked.

HEAT THE WAX.

Drip on envelope.

Press with seal.

Dust with sand.

Tap away excess. *Lightly.*

Aless glanced about his chamber and let out the steady stream of air he hadn't realized he'd been holding. Completed. He held up the envelope and considered the consequences of the events he was poised to set in motion. His gaze moved to the bell pull. Once this missive left his hands 'twould be no going back.

'Twas his duty to send it, if only to justify his father's recent decent into unmitigated madness. Aless swallowed. He must. As madness was the only rational account that would explain the Conte's aberrant remarks on Chalmers having been snatched from his clutches. But in all reality, how far was his father likely to push? The Conte's sudden decline had a dangerous undercurrent that sent an apprehensive chill over Aless. Not to mentions his hopes of furthering an effort with Lady Esmeralda.

Aless pushed the thoughts away. His father would not dare do something so foolish. The people of Chalmers were their allies, for God's sake.

But why the clandestine meetings? The secrecy?

Aless considered the set of the Conte's shoulders the prior day, his clenched fists, his ramblings on *magic dust*...Truly, his father had crossed over the edge of sanity. Perhaps most disturbing was his father's purpose in demanding his sudden marriage? And not just his own, but Niccòlo's as well.

Duty, of course. It all came down to duty.

Still, there were questions. He tapped the envelope on the secretary in one last deliberating effort before tugging the bell pull. Decision made.

Seconds later a soft knock sounded at the door. "Enter," he barked.

"Sir?"

Alessandro thrust the missive at the servant before he wavered any further. "See that this is dispatched immediately."

"ARE YOU CERTAIN YOU know where you are going? Mayhap, we should have requested a driver?" Essie asked softly. The rutted road tossed Essie and Cill about haphazardly, sending each of them perilously close to being pitched over the side. She just prayed Cill's constitution was up to the challenge. But the small carriage never slowed.

"Cinde, how did you learn of this Pinetti?" Cill demanded.

"Quit biting her head off, Cill," Essie said. "I vow, you should be knighted Sir Grouse." Essie shot her a sly smile. "In less than a week, she could order you beheaded." Of course it mattered for naught, as was obvious by the roll of Cinde's eyes heavenward.

Cinde ignored both hers and Cill's outburst and flicked the reins, and said mildly, "We are on the right path."

There was much to admire Cinde's skill in avoidance of the petty bickering, and her driving. Prince would have fits if he discovered them.

Essie let out a sigh. Her gloomy thoughts were getting worse. Not many girls of her age and station had to deal with the embarrassment of batting eyes and a domineering Maman.

"I spoke to Manette. She was more than helpful," Cinde said.

Though the day had started out in brilliant sunrise, ominous clouds were rising quickly, promising an eventful ride home. There was not much time to lose.

"Pinetti is not French in origin, is he?" Cill asked.

"I believe he is Italian."

"Interesting that, all the Italians running about, *oui*?" Essie murmured. Tall trees softened shadows over their path as the clouds continued to gather. The lined road was a rugged one that had her jaw aching. A sudden thought occurred. "Do you suppose he is related to the de Lecces?" she frowned.

Cill's glance in her direction spelled plainly she thought the question ridiculous.

"What? I know not every Italian is related to every other Italian, but it's possible *they* are related."

Again, Cinde managed to stifle the growing antagonism by intervening, something Essie noticed Cinde was becoming quite efficient in. "The de Lecces' nobility would have them frequenting the theatre, I imagine," Cinde said. "They are certainly more than likely acquainted."

"How is it that he lives here?" Cill asked.

"I don't know but it has been many years, according to Manette."

"Manette is but all of sixteen," Cill pointed out.

Cinde laughed. "*Mais oui*, but her Maman and grand-mère, and so on, have been here nigh on generations. He is quite mysterious she said, and somewhat...um...testy."

"I've read about Chevalier Joseph Pinetti," Essie said. "I believe he's made quite the stir across the continent."

"Surely, he cannot be the same man," Cill mused. "I, too, have heard talk on that particular Pinetti. He is known as the 'Professor of Natural Magic.' If it is he, we shall be lucky indeed to find him in residence."

"We shall know soon enough," Cinde said.

Essie thought her words cryptic, but held her tongue. Cinde had a surprising stubborn streak of which not many people were aware. She presented a most amiable demeanor. Ha!

"If I am not mistaken, this is the forked path where we veer left. His cottage should be just round the bend." A swoop of wind gusts swirled dried leaves, dirt, and other indistinguishable debris up from the ground in perfect symmetrical spirals that led a path straight to the mysterious magician's door.

Essie took that to be a sign. Good or bad, remained to be seen.

Chapter 8

"HAS PADRE SPOKEN TO YOU, Niccòlo?" Alessandro browsed the bookcase without seeing a single title, hands clasped at his lower back. Despite weak streams of morning sunbeams piercing the lace curtains, the library felt gloomy. Perhaps it was his mood.

"Regarding?"

Aless turned and faced his younger brother whose features closely favored his own. Fiercely intelligent eyes sparked with a rebellion Alessandro found amusing. 'Twas not so long ago he'd sported that same fire. In point of fact, as recently as the eve before. That thought brought his amusement up short.

A warming fire burned in the hearth and kept the cool morning at bay. Aless moved to the windows and pushed aside the lace linings. Storm clouds gathered in the distance, not unlike his careening thoughts.

"Our heritage," he said slowly.

"What the devil are you on about, Aless?" It was apparent Niccòlo was sore regarding some matter, and determined to lay the blame at Aless's feet. Definitely pouting.

"Of my impending marital obligations."

That succeeded in garnering Niccòlo's attentions. "Impending ma-marital obligations?"

"*Sì.*"

"But, who—" Niccòlo's eyes narrowed on him.

" 'Who' does not matter." Aless focused on the toe of his boots before glancing up. "What does matter, however, is this sudden obligation."

"Sudden obligation?" Niccòlo cracked a sudden grin. "Well, my brother, you are soon to cross the thirty mark, sì? Quite the old man."

Alessandro shot him a scowl that, under other circumstances, would have had his younger brother challenging him for a good old-fashioned physical bout. Before he could scrape together any scathing words, the library door swung wide.

Lady Kendra beamed a blinding smile in Aless's direction, her father following leisurely behind. The determined glint in her eye had Aless mustering a quick smile in an effort to hide a groan. One would have thought Aless held up a red cape at her sudden charge in his direction—with no hope of escape.

An eager Niccòlo leaped to his feet. Ah, so that was the way of it. It shed a new angle on the entire situation. There was enough ornery sibling rivalry in Aless to have him biting the inside of his cheek to keep from laughing outright.

The tension in Niccòlo's jaw as he pulled to an abrupt halt was well worth the entertainment value. Even if Aless had had the opportunity to allay his brother's insecurities in that arena, Aless doubted he would have done so. It was much too fun to poke at his younger brother after that unkind remark on his majority.

Lady Kendra swooped in like a hawk and clasped Alessandro's arm, talons notwithstanding.

"Lady Kendra," he acknowledged—as if he'd had any other option. He hoped he did not sound as choked as he felt.

Her apple green dress, brighter than the sun, over compensated for the darkened clouds beyond the windows. Lacy trim—Belgian, no doubt—edged the somewhat plunging neckline. Alessandro let go of the grin he'd been holding back at the sight of Niccòlo's compressed lips.

"Signore de Lecce," she said breathlessly. "I understand there is to be an archery contest of sorts on the morrow."

"*Sí, Signorina.* I had heard that as well."

"Croquet, this afternoon."

"*Sí.*"

"Will you be competing, *Signore*?" Her twittering reminded him of a canary. "My father is quite skilled, you know."

"Is he?" Alessandro murmured. The imposing earl cast a grim smile his way and the collar around Alessandro's neck seemed to tighten.

"I shall champion your every effort, my lord." Her pale eyes fluttered in a wispy...and, err...flirtatious manner.

He cast a veiled glance toward the curtains at the windows, away from Niccòlo's black scowl.

Just as he'd thought, not a flicker of movement.

"'TIS QUITE EERIE, *NON*?" Cinde said. Her voice barely rose above a whisper.

Essie swallowed, gaze riveted by swirling dirt not of her doing. Trees rustled in a gentle wind that she knew from experience failed to create the odd phenomenon. Truly fascinating. She wondered if she might conquer something of that nature with a little practice. She'd never considered her affliction as an asset before. The velocity of the shift in updraft sent a tingle up her spine.

"Essie!" She started at Cill's sharp tone.

"W-what?" But before Cill blast her with any snide remarks, the door to the thatched-roof hut jerked open, revealing a very short, very elderly gentleman, almost troll-like in stature. His chin would not have reached Essie's shoulder if he'd stood on the tips of his toes. Unruly, gray hair spiked in all directions. A pointy nose and thinned lips did not bode well for the three of them.

"Chevalier Pinetti?" Cinde asked. Her polite tone held a slight edge.

"*Oui, oui.* What is this about? You are disturbing the sublime semblance of spherical balance in the realm of my meager existence. Ze cosmos will react violently."

"Our apologies, *Monsieur.* We do not wish to disturb the cosmos."

"Then be gone, all of you," he roared. His tiny body blast a force of energy of the like of which Essie had never witnessed. Shrewd blue eyes sparkled insidiously, drawing attention away from any other unsightly features his aging face may have held. Those eyes held Essie's gaze riveted by their fathomless depths. Pools of swirling embers threatened to erupt, or cast some ghastly hex over the lot of them.

Mon...Dieu, Essie breathed. Cill stepped forward. Essie, however, took a reverse step, recognizing all signs of her sister's ire.

"I say, sir, heed how you speak to the Princess of Chalmers." Cill's voice, hard and demanding, showed not even a twinge of fear. Essie would not mind commanding that tone on occasion. 'Twas quite admirable.

The odd-looking man froze; lanced Cinde with a glare that stole Essie's breath—or in Essie's case— sent her eyes fluttering in a burst. Spirals of dirt rose into cyclonic proportions another two feet from the ground. Suffice to say it gleaned his attention, but only for a second. Those hypnotic eyes pierced Cinde again. Essie could not have spoken had someone held a dagger at her throat.

"Eh?" he said. "Princess, you say?" He cocked his head to one side, his gaze intent and unrelenting. Cinde straightened her shoulders and faced him squarely.

Essie blinked once trying to gain calm before she wreaked undue havoc in the weather, rather worsening their situation. She ached to bask in Cill and Cinde's confidence, but she was too frightened.

"*Mais oui, Monsieur.*" Cinde gave a stately incline of her head. She certainly made good use of her noble learnings.

To Essie's surprise, the old man chuckled. Cackled, more like. Essie glanced at Cill who appeared just as puzzled as she felt.

"Come in, my child. Ze work I did on you..." He kissed the tips of his fingers. "*Voilà.* I could not have been more pleased."

"*You?*" Cinde gasped. "You are my fairy godmother?"

He turned and strode to the door of the cottage, unmindful he'd left the three of them standing in his...dust. "Bah, she is but my agent," Chevalier Pinetti said impatiently, Cinde and Cill fast on his heels. Essie hurried after her sisters.

"She?" Essie and Cill said. "Who is *she?*" Cill asked, but Chevalier Pinetti either did not, or chose not, to hear and disappeared inside.

Essie stepped across the threshold into a barren room, housing one small table flanked by two chairs on dirt floors. An unusual odor touched the air. Essie wrinkled her nose and resisted an urge to breathe through the sleeve of her gown. A pit in the center of the room had the flames of a small fire licking the bottom of a large black pot. Swirls of smoke formed an 's' toward the ceiling, dissipating into nothingness. A shiver of fear pricked her skin.

"You are the stage magician?" By silent agreement Cinde seemed their best candidate as spokesperson.

"Bah, that trickster! He knows not what he is about."

"Grandfather, you shall have your guests doubting my abilities with such talk." Amusement colored a deep voice that resonated through the small hut, startling Essie.

She edged closer to Cill, eyes fastened on the darkened corner. Unable to stifle her battering eyes in a flurry of nerves, the fire leaped with the surge of oxygen.

Mystery solved, almost, as he stepped from the shadows. Tall, elegant, slender—a man fashioned for the stage. Deep, familiar blue eyes pierced them, and a quirk to his lips that surely had audiences swooning. Most notably were his strong capable hands and broad shoulders.

"Ladies," he drawled in a voice full of velvet warmth. "Chevalier Joseph Pinetti, *the third* at your service." His bow was deep and flourished. Essie heard a suspicious snort from Cill's direction...but...surely not. Essie could scarcely breathe. The man was lethally attractive.

"I suppose I must lay claim to the blackguard," the elderly Pinetti spat. "He comes home only for the coronation ceremony. Useless. He is but useless." His mutterings indicated he'd forgotten Essie and her sisters.

"Sir, about the fairy godmother," Essie said. Two sets of piercing blues, scrutinizing, had her voice shifting into an unnatural octave. Her eyes sputtered into action.

"Eh?" His bushy brows leaped above his forehead. "What about her?"

"W-we were h-hoping you might help us in d-determining the rules of her magic. Is there...there p-perchance a...a rule-b-book?"

"*A rulebook!*" For such a tiny man his voice rattled the walls of the little cottage.

Essie flinched but found she could not drag her eyes from Pinetti's very distracting grandson. His hand twisted in one smooth fluid motion and a book appeared from nowhere. She gasped again, blinking furiously. The pages ruffled in the wake of another sudden indoor windstorm.

"Bah! Give me that, you silly boy." The gnarled hand snatched the book from his grandson's clasp. "'Tis naught but my old sorcerer's recipes. I don't know how I hold my head up around you. Tricks...just silly parlor tricks," he muttered. He tossed the offending tome in the corner.

"What do you want with *rules*?" His impatience unnerved her, which of course, brought the draft to higher proportions.

The younger Pinetti seemed unfazed. He just stared at her, rendering her immobile. "Incredible," he said softly, his hand reaching forward.

Cill stepped in front of Essie breaking his mesmeric hold. But she addressed the older Pinetti. "Sir, we beg you of your expertise—"

"I-I..." Essie glanced at the younger man, her words faltering. She inhaled deeply. It was now or never. "Y-you see, I have th-this affliction."

The old man shuffled his way forward and peered up at her. Agonizing silence filled the small room, all breath ceased. Her fluttering eyes increased in velocity under the intense scrutiny. "Bah! 'tis something you will control in time. Be gone, all of you." He moved to the pot and stirred whatever concoction it contained. You—" He pointed to his grandson. "—as well."

Tears filled Essie's eyes as hope flickered from her like a doused flame.

The younger man threw out his hands in surrender, palms up. "Grandfather, you shall break my hardened heart with such talk."

The old man looked over at Cinde. "Not you, my dear. *You* may stay." He gave her a winsome smile. "*You* are my work of art, you see."

"W-w-work of a-art?"

Chapter 9

LADY KENDRA FRAZIER WAS a work of art, Aless decided—the quintessential Renaissance painting with her head tilted just so, as if she were...on display.

Aless looked up at the leaden sky to hide his frustration. The Conte was proving relentless in his determination in pairing him with Lady Kendra. His father had turned a charming smile on her that rivaled that of the future king of Chalmers, all the while heralding the two of them through the terrace doors for a morning of "fresh air." She'd blushed furiously while Aless hid his exasperation behind a grim smile.

He studied her slender form and delicate demeanor. It was impossible to find fault with her physique or manner. His father was right—she was everything *proper*. The over-bright dress she wore almost brought tears to his eyes. And the knowledge that she portrayed perfect wifely material *did* bring tears to his eyes.

"I vow the morning air is just the thing," she twittered.

He resisted an urge to roll his eyes. Such dazzling and twittering this early in the morn could do serious damage to one's constitution. Augh...when had he become so cynical? "*Sì, Signorina.*"

"I do believe we are in for some wet weather."

"*Sì.*" He struggled for something less inane than the climate on which to comment. But no, he had nothing. Clopping of horse hooves on gravel spared him.

"Oh, my," she breathed. "Where do you suppose the sisters were this morning? Is that the *princess*? In such a...a plain contraption—*driving*?"

Alessandro shifted his gaze over the field to the small opened-top carriage, where indeed, Ladies Pricilla and Esmeralda seemed to be holding on for dear life as Princess Cinderella snapped the reins, compelling a faster trot. *Dio.* They were liable to break their fool necks at that speed. Even from this distance he could sense the underlying excitement in their faces. He had a feeling it had nothing to do with the scheduled croquet festivities planned post luncheon.

As the carriage drew nearer, he found himself riveted by the brilliance in Lady Esmeralda's eyes. Quite striking when one had an opportunity to observe her without her nerves nourishing a change in atmospheric conditions. She wore a soft yellow gown that shifted the gloom-filled skies into that of a warm summer afternoon.

"What has you smiling so, my lord?" The shrill edge in Lady Kendra's tone startled him. La! Saved by Prince Charming and Sir Arnald. The two men rushed forward, coinciding with the arrival of the carriage.

"Might I inquire as to where you ladies have been?" Prince asked, mildly. The tone warred with his tensed jaw. Aless bit back a grin. Prince Charming was furious. He had Aless's sympathies.

"I vow this brisk wind has done wonders for me this morning," Lady Pricilla said.

Her announcement hadn't fooled anyone as a distraction. But distraction from what, pray tell? His lips twitched when he caught sight of the glare Lady Esmeralda shot her.

"How wonderful to see you, my husband. I thought the men were to hunt pheasants this morning," Princess Cinderella smiled. She'd pointedly ignored her husband's query of their whereabouts.

"We did," he said flatly.

It did not take a woman's intuition for Aless to realize that was a conversation that would continue in private. He also knew that something more than brisk wind had something to do with Lady Esmeralda's flushed appearance and fluttering eyes. There was a glittering fury emanating from her that had him more than curious.

"The air certainly seems to have agreed with *you*, my dear." Arnald stepped up and assisted Lady Pricilla from the carriage. Unlike the prince, Arnald was more amused than annoyed, which flabbergasted Aless, considering the breakneck speed he'd just witnessed.

Lady Esmeralda's next words sent a jolt of irritation through Aless. "We met the most amazing elderly little man," she said.

"Is that so?" Prince Charming's tone turned somewhat ominous, but no one appeared to heed the warning.

"*Mais oui.* Chevalier Joseph Pinetti."

"Elderly? Pinetti!" Alessandro sputtered. "That fraud? Nor is he so little."

"So you *do* know him. We wondered, of course." Lady Esmeralda pulled herself to full height, entertainingly so. Right up to the top of Alessandro's chin, sparing him a single glance of aggravation. "You must be speaking of his grandson. He was there as well. Why, he conjured a book straight from mid-air." Her hand fluttered out, demonstrating. "How do *you* know of him, *Signore*?" Lady Esmeralda asked.

"We were at school together," Alessandro informed her blandly. "He is widely traveled as a *stage* magician." His tone rang fanned the courtyard. He felt the curiosity of several pairs of eyes and the heat up his neck.

"Ah, very good," Princess Cinderella said. "I've requested his attendance at the coronation ceremony. In fact, I took the liberty of inviting him for the rest of the week's festivities."

"What?" Alessandro's question blended with Sir Arnald's and the prince's unrestrained groans. For once it seemed all three men were in accord. Over the course of the last few years those times were few indeed. The fact that they all were in some sort of silent alignment regarding Pinetti spelled trouble to Aless.

Thus far Lady Kendra had remained unnaturally silent. Based on her narrowed gaze, however, he could see she weighed every spoken word. She may be young, Aless thought, but she if was savvy enough to navigate the London ballrooms then she, more than most, had a greater understanding of innuendos and political undercurrents in social situations.

"My dear princess, may I remind you there is a croquet match after lunch we are to attend?" Prince said. Aless read the underlying words as *'My dear wife, may-I-remind-you-you-are-the-future-queen-and-you-are-not-to-drive-a-carriage-like-a-bat-out-of-hell.'*

"Of course, my dear." She gave them all a brilliant smile. "My wager is on Pricilla."

"Mine, as well," Lady Esmeralda chimed in, drawing an indelicate snort from Lady Pricilla.

Aless had known the sisters long enough to realize *he* would not be wagering against Lady Pricilla. Surprisingly, Lady Kendra's social cues in this instant seemed to desert her. "My money is on Signore de Lecce," she said. All eyes shifted to him then her. "He has agreed to partner me in the games."

Well, he thought, maintaining a bland expression at that blatant untruth, nothing more stimulating than an afternoon sport of Bloodbath.

Without further warning, the darkened clouds unleashed a rash of torrent rains.

Perfect.

Chapter 10

"HOW SHALL WE MANAGE to get through the afternoon?" Essie scowled. "There will be no croquet with this deluge. I was quite looking forward to putting Mistress Priss in her place." Essie couldn't quite understand her hypersensitivity with the quaint and beautiful, *un*-batting-eyed Kendra, but the English miss was an irritant, somewhat like a small pebble in one's shoe. Essie let out a breath. Leastways, more guests were arriving hourly, so she and her sisters would not be required to entertain the brat for hours on end much longer.

Staring out the windows, Essie could hardly see the pond across the gardens for the blackened skies and blinding rain. She turned and meandered over to where Cinde and Cill sat drinking their tea. She perched herself on the arm of Cill's chair.

Cinde had done a fabulous job revamping her former bed chamber into a sitting room of sorts. One of the many rewards, Cinde had informed them, in her position as Princess Charming.

To which they'd all burst into fits of laughter. Oh, the memories.

Soft greens and cream carried a feeling of spring, most especially with a warm fire blazing in the hearth. Fresh scented flowers—Manette, the culprit—completed the effect. They'd used the chamber for nigh on four and a half years now, since Cinde's nuptials to Prince Charming.

There was less likely the threat of Maman's intrusion. By unspoken rule none of the three saw fit to mention their secluded hideaway. The posted guard at the end of the entry hall assured those efforts.

"Mistress Priss?" Cill choked out a laugh. "Careful, Ess, you sound almost green with envy."

"Envy! Of that little...little—"

"I vow, we barely escaped with our lives this morning," Cinde interrupted, with a delicate shudder. "'Twas a close call, indeed."

"That is somewhat of an overstatement, *non*?" Essie said.

"I'm speaking of our husbands," she retorted.

Essie glowered at her, but it went unnoticed. "I don't have a husband."

"You know what I mean." Cinde offered up a benign smile.

Essie opened her mouth to respond, but snapped it shut instead. She drew in a deep breath and asked the dreaded question. "What are you going to tell Prince? He will demand to know." Essie hated the idea of her sisters discussing her unfavorable eye condition with them. It was beyond humiliating.

"Mayhap, I will have to say nothing," she said.

Essie frowned. "I don't understand."

"Don't you?" Cinde asked softly, smiling.

Essie glanced over at Cill, but she had the same ridiculous smile on her face. A smile full of secrets.

Essie desperately wanted to succumb to pettiness out of frustration, but that never did any good. "*Monsieur* Pinetti is quite intimidating," she said instead.

"He's just an old man set in his ways," Cinde defended. "I was quite taken with him."

Essie fingered the lace cuff of one sleeve. "I was speaking of his grandson."

"Oh."

Essie heard the grin in Cinde's tone and felt the heat rise in her cheeks. She jumped up and stalked back to the windows where splattering raindrops plopped against the glass like huge tears. "This rain is spoiling everything."

Cill grimaced. "I daresay we shall be forced to play charades."

Essie cheered at that, she loved charades. Her acting skills far exceeded that of her sisters. Surely, she should be able to waylay the fair Lady Kendra. "*Oui.* Charades should pass the time nicely." She clapped her hands together and skipped back to her sisters. Things were looking up.

"Alas, I do not have to play charades," Cinde said, smugly. After a short pause, she frowned.

Though Essie was disappointed, she was compelled to ask, "What is it, Cinde?"

"Nothing, I suppose. Prince and I are spending a day or two with Prince Reynardo of Spain, and his wife, Inez."

Essie gazed at her thoughtfully. "Why should that worry you?"

"Worry me?" Cinde flicked a piece of lint from her skirt.

"We know you too well, *ma chère.* You are worried, *non?*

"Mayhap a little."

"Don't tell me it revolves around that little incident of smuggled goods Cill and Sir Arnald stumbled across. That was four years ago," Essie said.

"The problem with that 'little incident' you so glibly label, Essie," Cill said, eyes closed, head back, "is that a large portion of those smuggled goods included a cave full of loaded arms. Not to mention barrels of black powder."

Essie sank down on the settee across from Cinde. "And you think that your visits with the Spanish Royalty will accomplish—"

"—*maintain* an important alliance," she corrected grimly.

"Personally, I prefer a nap," Cill said. "I do not feel so well. I vow the lamb at lunch was unbearable."

"But you love lamb," Essie frowned.

"Obviously, not today," she said.

ESSIE RAN HER FINGERS over an imaginary pet, taming him. It was all so simple. She was, after all, excellent at Charades. She studied the small crowd of people in the room. The younger members of the group were gathered in an inner circle that included Cill, Alessandro, his brother Niccòlo, Lady Kendra, and a couple of newcomers who'd recently arrived, Lady Brigitte and Joseph Pinetti. The outer circle served up Maman's disapproving scowl, the queen, and her twin sisters', indulgent smile. A diverse audience.

"What on earth are you doing?" Cill grumbled.

Essie pressed her lips together and glared at her ill-tempered sister. Obviously Essie was handling her pantomime all wrong. She had half a mind to point to Cill for the fourth word—*Shrew*. But in light of Cill's obvious distress of late, Essie discarded that idea, rather tapping her foot in search for other inspiration.

Ha! She touched her thumbs together, palms out to peer at her audience through a makeshift two-dimensional square. She pasted on a brilliant smile for added benefit. 'Twas a tough crowd. She seemed to be the only one enjoying herself.

"Frame?" Niccòlo de Lecce called out.

Essie thought him adorable, if a bit young. Too bad he and his brother looked so alike. No doubt they age would gracefully, if one based outcomes on the

Conte's appearance. Truly a detriment per Alessandro's heartfelt sentiments, so eloquently expressed in his little tête-à-tête with his *Papa*. Whom she also wished to the devil.

Pointing at Niccòlo, she nodded quickly. She then drew a motion with her index finger and thumb on one hand, touching the air across, indicating length to the word.

"Frame-ing?" Niccòlo said. Slowly this time.

She tugged on her ear.

"Sounds like?"

Oh, he was good. She nodded, grinning her approval. Signore de Lecce, *Alessandro,* shot his brother a scowl, but ignored their silly undercurrents.

"Flaming?" Lady Brigitte.

She shook her head.

"Claiming?" Lady Kendra.

Non. Frustrated, she almost stomped her foot in frustration. Instead, she pressed her lips together lest any sound tried to escape. The rules were quite explicit.

"Training!" Monsieur Pinetti.

Cill let out an exaggerated sigh. "Taming," she said, clearly bored, and not at all in the spirit of the game. "The Taming of the Shrew."

"*Mais oui!*" Essie dropped into a plush chair, spent. Barely a second passed before Joseph Pinetti bowed before her—elegant hands offering her a glass of lemonade. She choked back a startled gasp.

"*Mademoiselle?*" His voice, as smooth as velvet, dipped low, sending ripples up her spine.

Flamed heat rose up her neck. The flutter of panic tickled her nerve endings. He was just so...so attractive. "*M-m-erci, Monsieur.*" She accepted the glass, praying didn't disgrace herself by dropping it. She smiled quickly and lowered her eyes, willing them steady. He was a most unsettling man. Not a good combination for someone with her unfortunate affliction.

Once he stepped a proper distance away, she peered at him from beneath lowered lashes with a touch of melancholy. His grandfather pronounced the lack of a cure—said the control would be of her own making. It all sounded so reasonable when he'd sputtered the information with his thin arms flailing about.

Now, in the lighted parlor it all seemed so hopeless again. She sank deeper into her chair. Their little jaunt that morning had been a complete and useless waste of time after all. She glanced back up at Monsieur Pinetti and sighed.

He caught her eye and winked. A breathless surprise filled her. The beginnings of her lashes started to flutter. But she clamped her eyes shut and inhaled, deep. After a short pause she risked another glance his way and saw his lips twitch, unmistakably holding back a smile. An infectious euphoria flooded her and she found herself returning his grin. "'Tis your turn, Cill," she said, her voice breathy, gaze never wavering from Monsieur Pinetti.

Cill said, "I say, Monsieur Pinetti, we should consider it a great privilege to see *you* perform."

Aggravated, Essie bit her tongue glanced about the room. An unmistakable frown covered Alessandro de Lecce's handsome face. The sight appeased her some until she caught the Mistress Priss smiling like the cat that had swallowed the cream. Lady Brigitte's gloved fingers covered a wide smile.

"Oh, that's a brilliant idea," Alessandro smirked.

Essie scowled at Alessandro. What did he have to be so angry about? Despite Cill's manipulation, Essie couldn't deny the tingle of thrill that skittered over her skin. A murmur of approval rippled through the room. Even Lady Kendra shifted her attention at the request.

Monsieur Pinetti stood and looked in Essie's direction. He seemed to be waiting on some indication from *her*. She cleared her throat with a delicate cough, mayhap reveling in the attention a teeny bit.

"*Mais oui, s'il vous plaît, Monsieur*," she demurred, glancing about.

"We can play Charades anytime," Cill said.

Another disapproving frown deepened Alessandro's firm lips. And when Maman's scowl echoed his disapproval, Essie concurred. *They could play Charades anytime.*

CHEVALIER JOSEPH PINETTI, Viscount Lawrie, had stooped low. He may be Aless's friend, but today he rivaled his worst enemy. Rumors surrounding his interests in the dark arts made Joseph lively entertainment throughout the continent. And Aless knew better than most. Having attended school together from a young age they knew each other very well. But his blatant flattery toward Lady Esmeralda bordered on outrageous. He was flirting with like a seasoned suitor. And she an untried miss. It was despicable.

Irritation clawed his gut. He tried to shove away the unfamiliar sensations, telling himself he was just looking out for her; that she was unused to such shameless tactics. But she was eating up every glance, every *word*. His fist clenched at his side as he watched his old friend speak softly to a young servant boy. Aless couldn't discern the exchange but as least Joseph's attention had shifted from Lady Esmeralda. He let out a held breath, and loosened his fist.

Incredibly, Joseph seemed to pin the child with a searing look. Not unlike the one Aless had experienced from Sir Arnald's all those years ago.

The child appeared almost helpless under Joseph's intensive gaze, and Aless had half a mind to storm over and shake some sense into the child. The talk of mind control science was relatively new, and the popularity of it was taking hold across the continent. 'Twas one of those forbidden fruits young people were obsessed with. He winced. Mayhap, he *was* turning into his dear elderly *padre* at the ripe old age of thirty.

But then Joseph turned back to a smiling Lady Esmeralda and Aless's fist clenched again. Her enthrallment of Joseph's chicanery was infuriating. Surely anyone with eyes could see right through the *bastardo's* deceitful attentions. Jaw clamped, Aless had given her much more credit for her intelligence. She was not responisible, he decided, as his gaze drifted back to the child sitting quietly in the corner to await whatever Joseph had compell—

Aless leaned forward. What the hell was his angle? Could Joseph be trying get closer to the throne? Through *her*. It was beyond honorable. Mayhap his old friend had changed. If Joseph did not hesitate to ply his wiles on the young and innocents, was Lady Esmeralda no exception?

Typical of stage personas. They were not to be trusted. Out of nowhere another thread teased the edge of his...*Dio*. If Joseph thought to impel... no! Aless rubbed his fist with his other hand, tempted to plant it in Joseph's face. A black eye or two might teach the *bastardo*...Why, he would expose the fraud this instant.

He stood quickly, but something held him back, snagging his arm. He glanced down, surprised to see Lady Kendra smiling up at him to disguise her bewilderment. Aless glanced back up and saw Joseph moving away from Lady Esmeralda. He let out a rush of air and slowly lowered himself back down.

"Are you quite alright, *Signore*?" Lady Kendra asked softly.

"*Sí, sí*," he whispered a little impatiently.

She frowned in Joseph's direction. "I've met his father, the Earl, of course," she said. "Though never Lord Lawrie. He was always away—on stage as I understand it. Both of our fathers served in the House of Lords."

"Not many people realize his noble bloodlines," he said.

"I wonder why that is."

"...Dim the lights, if you please," Joseph said.

Lady Kendra sat up straight, leaned forward, but never relinquished her hold. Aless could feel his cravat tightening.

Joseph's voice alone created an ambience of anticipation, and an excited hush fell over the room as servants rushed about to do as he bid.

A chill crept up Alessandro's spine. A premonition of sorts.

Chapter 11

CONTE DE LECCE LIVED with few regrets, but alas, he loathed to admit, he may have made a grave mistake in confiding in his elder son. Honor was all well and good, but misplaced, it spelled nothing short of disaster. It pained him to think of the sacrifices he might be forced to execute.

The confines of the deserted chamber were stifling. Awaiting word from the captain of the small army he had in place, torture. Years, he'd bided his time. Now the throne was within an arm's reach, his dreams soon to be realized. Pasquale refused to pace. Pacing dredged up visions of a nervous man on the brink of his first liaison. Much was at stake.

He stepped to the window and gazed out over what would finally be his within days. His hands trembled with anticipation. Miles of valleys, sculpted gardens, farmed land—

"Sire." Sure, quick steps had eased into the chamber.

Pasquale turned. Lopé looked and moved just as his name implied, wolfish, with watchful yellowed eyes. His hair grew straight out from head like a strange, wire-haired pet, his stature small and sinewy. A man who could easily infiltrate and disappear quickly when needed.

"I've been waiting," Pasquale snapped.

Lopé's sharp, shallow bow should be deeper, show proper respect. Pasquale vowed that would change once he governed his new kingdom. He would be a tough taskmaster, yet fair. But loyalty—

demanded, first and foremost, lest risking severe punishment worthy of the dark ages.

"*Le mie scuse,* my apologies." A flash of fear touched Lopé's gaze.

Satisfied, Pasquale inclined his head in quick acquiescence. He cast a suspicious gaze about the chamber searching for signs of shimmers in the air but all he could detect were dust moats dancing before a bared window of gray skies. He was safe for the moment. "We've but a few days. All is in position?"

"*Sí,* sire," he said with another slight incline of his head.

"The child?"

"Our plans are in place."

"*Bueno.* Good," he said, rubbing his hands together, lingering doubts quelled.

Chapter 12

FIRELIGHT FLICKERED IN A sinister, opiate-inducing lethargy. A strategically placed mirror reflected the silver-gray skies through slightly parted drapes. The flash of periodic lightning greatly assisted Joseph's enthrall—a magician captivating his audience.

The man was insultingly charismatic, to Aless's innate disgust. He slid a glance about the room restraining a snort at the audience's gullibility. His gaze lingered on Lady Roche, Lady Esmeralda's large maman. She and Lady Kendra appeared to be the only two individuals unconvinced by Joseph's theatrics. Lady Kendra's knowledge of Joseph's world-wide theatrics raised her esteem a notch.

Lady Roche, however—well, he would not have credited her with that much sense. Aless watched her train narrowed eyes on Joseph, cognizant of the subtle attentions he portrayed toward her daughter.

Aless could read her thoughts as if she'd spoken them aloud—*it would not be born*, she seemed to vow. *The man was no better than an actor.* Which had another unnerving affect on Aless—raising his hackles in defense of his longtime friend. How would she feel knowing the man was in line for an earldom? Aless bit back a burst of laugher.

Then something truly odd happened. Lady Roche gazed at a blank spot on the Persian throw beneath her feet, gasped, then jerked her head up. She darted a sharp glance about, then froze when her eyes met Aless's. He offered a small smile and an incline of his head, before forcing his attention back on Joseph. A flicker of apprehension rippled over his skin, and he kept a heedful watch on her from his peripheral vision.

After a moment, her focus drifted back to that area on the rug and she nodded. Her eyes squinted and lips moved before finally blinking. She raised her eyes, snapping Lady Esmeralda from her reverie, who frowned at her mother.

It all played out as some badly written stage farce for which London patrons would have lunged rotten vegetables.

The instant Lady Esmeralda turned back to the other *farce* being played out, she was once again quickly absorbed. Aless pressed his lips together and vowed silently, Joseph would *not* be in the running for Lady Esmeralda's affections. Aless would see to that, and refused to look deeper into the whys.

From the corner of his eye, the tension surrounding Lady Roche flowed away like a wave back to sea. When she relaxed against her chair trepidation thrummed through him.

The rest of the company could not seem to keep their attention from Joseph's captivating presentation. He lifted a cloth from his hand and A spray of brilliant summer flowers appeared, though they were well into fall. The oohs and ahs were hushed, yet dazzled, by this ostentatious show. Ha! Child's play.

A stunned Lady Kendra sat next to him, hands clenched in her lap before her lips pressed into a tight grimace. But then Joseph had the unmitigated gall to step forward, and with an elegant bow, handed the luscious bouquet to Lady Esmeralda. Relief settled over Lady Kendra like a warm blanket, whose fingers loosened.

Aless's trepidation was suddenly replaced by a surge of fury.

THE SILENCE THAT BLARED through the chamber when Monsieur Pinetti bowed low before Essie had her wanting to fall through the floor. But she reached out with trembling fingers and accepted the small bunch of posies, face afire. Was he courting...*her?* She squeezed her eyes tight, if only to keep the windows from bursting forth and drenching them all, though the cool rain would not be remiss. She inhaled and slowly raised her eyes. With tilted lips, Monsieur Pinetti moved center stage once more.

Essie didn't even bother to struggle for indifference to the magician's fluid movements—movements that mesmerized the entire assemblage. 'Twas impossible besides. The atmosphere grew so palpable she thought she would rupture from the anticipation. She waited, spellbound.

"As you might be aware," Pinetti started. His deep resonance was ideal for the stage, and Essie could not stop the flutters in her stomach. She had the fleeting thought that perhaps he could mesmerize her affliction into nonexistence. "I am an illusionist. What that means, is that I can trick you into seeing things that are not really there. Let's try it, shall we?" He grinned at his audience, and Essie was certain Lady Brigitte was about to swoon. "Keep your eyes on the looking glass," he said. Those strong elegant hands lifted a large sheet of muslin from the mirror.

Nothing could prepare Essie for what happened next. A shadowed silhouetted profile of Edric, her dear, small Edric, appeared in the reflective glass. Essie's heart pounded so hard she dare not stand lest she faint dead away. The image wavered apart from the glass and rose similar to that of the flaming tips of fire.

Hand clutched at her chest, she barely heard the unified gasps. But the illusionist had not finished beguiling his audience. A small, high voice called out, "Help me."

A bloodcurdling scream pierced the shocked silence that had filled the room. All blood drained from Monsieur Pinetti's handsome face, who looked as stunned as anyone.

Essie hardly registered her mother's whipered words. *"Brava, Monsieur."*

She darted a glance at Maman, horrified someone other than she might have heard. And, despite Maman's cumbersome frame, Essie leaped from the settee. She wasn't certain who screamed but Cill had fainted. Completely *un*-Cill like, jarring Essie into motion. She was too late. Maman was pushing her way through the crowd where Cill lay in a heap on the floor.

All Essie could do was thank the heavens that Cinde and Prince were not present.

The attention shifted to the drama unfolding around Monsieur Pinetti where Sir Arnald held him by the scruff of his neck, barking out orders to one of the attendants manning the door. "Take him below."

"No!" Essie gasped. She fought her way through the crowd, but the chevalier was hauled away before she could reach them. She shook off someone's grip and squeezed her way past the rest of the throng into the hallway. Monsieur Pinetti was already disappearing round the corner. Another sudden thought ripped through her. *Edric!*

She would deal with Monsieur Pinetti's dilemma later, and ran all the way to the nursery. Panting, she shoved the door back so hard it bounded against the wall behind. The children! *Where were the children?*

"Edric," she called, sharply.

A startled nursemaid's head peered from the sitting room beyond. She held Arabella who gazed upon Essie, wide-eyed, thumb in her mouth.

Essie darted forward and held out her arms. Without the least bit of hesitation Bella reached for her. Essie cradled her head against her pounding heart. "Where is Edric?" she asked the now frazzled nursemaid.

"Here, Aunt Sessie." His fierce mien poked from behind his keeper's gray, bombazine skirts.

Essie let out a shaky breath, so relieved her knees tremble. "Thank God, Edric," she whispered.

DIO! ALESSANDRO LEAPED TO his feet scrambling to assist Joseph. The man was a menace to his own health. But a burly guard was already escorting him from the chamber. And in Lady Esmeralda's haste to escape, he was practically knocked on his arse. He clutched her arm, but she jerked free and vanished in the crowd.

Aless started after her when he caught the narrowed gaze and compressed lips of Lady Roche just as Arnald scooped his wife straight from the woman's bear-like paws. Lady Roche stood slowly— red-faced and humiliated, and veered after Lady Esmeralda.

On nothing other than instinct, Aless smoothly blocked her path. Beneath the archway he met another determined gaze. Lady Kendra. Two high spots of color dotted her otherwise pale façade. She was very angry, but Aless had no time to deal with her theatrics.

Lady Roche patted Lady Pricilla's hand, glancing surreptitiously at Arnald's implacable expression. Her demeanor quickly transposed to one of contriteness. Not her eyes, however. "Darling, you appear ashen. You are unwell?"

"*Non*, Maman. Just a bit fatigued is all."

Aless admired the stubborn tilt to Lady Pricilla's jaw and her husband's imposing stance at keeping her demons, rather *demon*, at bay. But there was something else. A niggle of suspicion that touched the nape of his neck. She had faked the entire scenario. Oh, not the illusion. Aless had witnessed Joseph's shock. If he was not mistaken, Lady Pricilla had fainted to create a diversion. A brilliant maneuver.

Aless had a sudden urge to find Lady Esmeralda. Was she party to this façade? He slipped past to the crowd into the corridor. But 'twas too late. Neither Joseph nor Lady Esmeralda was in sight. And Joseph was in dire straits.

Aless was flummoxed. How had Joseph accomplished it? Icy fingers of dread gripped his throat as a picture of that shadowed specter shuddered though his mind. That child's appearance begged for deliverance. But from what? The image too closely resembled the young prince. Ha! It was likely to have Joseph swinging from the gallows after such an asinine stunt. 'Twas a very foolish gimmick.

The whole presentation set Aless on edge. A trick of light and mirrors, that's all it was, he told himself. Then why did it feel more like an omen of doom? He stalked to the confines of his chamber, unsure of how to help his friend.

Sabato, his valet, was busy brushing out his dinner apparel.

"What say you, Sabato? Is our magician a fraud?" Aless, too anxious to sit, paced the chamber like a caged tiger.

"*Dio*, how would I know? I was not present, *sì?*" Aless bit back a grim smile at Sabato's impertinence. The man was old enough to be his grandfather, having been with the family since the dawn of time. His hair was thick and white, every strand in place, black eyes shrewd and observant. "Your pacing...'tis annoying."

Alessandro ignored him. There was surely no possible way he could go to the prince's cousin, most especially the prince. He'd be lucky if they didn't toss Aless in the dungeon with Joseph, if that was indeed where they'd stashed him. He surveyed the wide hall, vacant but for a servant or two. There must be someone he could implore for assistance. But the picture of Joseph's attentions on Lady Esmeralda prompted an irrational irritation, tempting him to just let Joseph stew in his own troubles.

He let out a sigh knowing he would not do that to his friend. Perhaps he should speak with Lady Esmeralda regarding the issue. A thought which cheered him immensely. Aless started towards the door.

"And where do suppose you are off to?" Sabato demanded.

"I—"

"You must dress for dinner. Monsieur Pinetti must wait."

"But—" Sabato's sharp gaze stopped Aless. And he realized there was something darker underfoot. He relented, turning to another matter, that deep in his gut, he was certain played a part. "Sabato, why is the Conte so insistent upon my sudden nuptials, do you suppose?"

"I've no idea. But 'tis time in my estimation, you are getting no younger, *sì*?"

"I am not so old," Alessandro grumbled.

"Ha! You need a nice Italian miss," he said.

"*Italian*," Alessandro repeated. But no Italian miss he knew had eyes so green they'd compete with the vibrant hills of Tuscany after a summer rain, fresh and sharp. Or copper tresses so rich that her allure grew in monumental proportions. Ironically, that unpredictable, nervous flutter Lady Esmeralda possessed acted as an interesting deterrent. He winced. Now, it seemed he couldn't keep visions of her filling his every waking moment.

The unexpected thoughts confused him and he shoved them away. And, now Joseph! He groaned. He must find a way to speak with the prince. Perhaps Sir Arnald's would be willing to assist...

"You will be late, Aless," Sabato informed him curtly. "Do not forget the missive that arrived for you while you were attending your parlor games."

"Missive? Why did you not say so?" He snatched an envelope from Sabato's outstretched hand and ripped it open and read through it quickly. "Who brought this, old man?"

Sabato sniffed. "Bah! I was not here when it arrived."

Aless let out a growl. "It appears my clandestine presence is once again required under the cover of darkness."

Chapter 13

ESSIE THOUGHT HER HEART would stop. It was seeing Bella and Edric safely in the confines of the nursery that finally slowed her thrumming pulse. She leaned against the wall just outside the children's room, hand on her chest.

Time to find Monsieur Pinetti. Whatever he'd been expecting to astound his audience with, she was most certain it was not the illusion of Edric crying out in a petrified voice. She'd seen his reaction.

As luck would have it, good or bad, Sir Arnald rounded the corner in her direction. She straightened away from the wall. "Ah, Sir Arnald. May I inquire as to what has become of the esteemed Monsieur Pinetti?"

"Esteemed?" The heat rose in her cheeks under his intense scrutiny. After a long pause, he finally said, "He is comfortably ensconced in his chamber, Lady Esmeralda."

"Oh."

A grim smile touched his lips and he lifted a brow. "You expected me to have him strapped to The Rack, no doubt."

"Well—"

"Not to worry, my dear, he is safe for the moment. But rest assure, I shall be keeping a close eye on him. He was quite impressive, *non*?"

"*Oui*," she whispered. She shook her head. "I don't know how he did it."

"Perhaps it will ease your mind if I tell you the fact that Pinetti seemed just as bewildered as the rest of us is what convinced me that that trick was not intended." He paused. "Praise saints my cousin nor his wife were present."

She agreed whole-heartedly with that sentiment. "How is Cill?"

"She is fine," he said gruffly. "For a moment there, I admit, I was quite terrified." His concern never failed to touch her. "I think she timed her swoon to perfection. What say you?"

"You think she pulled that stunt deliberately?" How like her over-dramatic sister.

He grinned. "I would not venture to say, my lady. Run along now, I shall see to your sister."

Essie shook her head and started down the corridor to her own suite of rooms. Unfortunately, not quickly enough.

"Might I beg a word with you, my darling?"

Nervous flutters reached more than Essie's eyes at Maman's steely demand. Anxiety twisted through her lower belly. "*Oui,* Maman," she said. Essie flashed an uneasy glance toward the nursery's closed door. Desperately, she searched her mind for what onerous deed she'd committed to warrant the unexpected hostility. But then, when Maman was about, how could the hostility be unexpected?

Maman slipped an arm through hers in a simulated friendly fashion. Oh, *non.* The error must have been truly egregious, indeed. She swallowed. "Is-is something amiss, Maman?" Essie failed miserably in quelling the turbulent flurry of air. Something Maman truly abhorred. Curtains lining large windows along the corridor stirred at the onset.

"I see we've yet to control your little problem." It was said pleasantly enough but 'twas what made Maman so dangerous. One who underestimated her natural tendency toward violence paid dearly. 'Twas lucky Essie had an answer for this one.

"*Non*, but w-we are working on a resolution," she said quickly.

"A resolution?"

"*Mais oui,* we spoke to-to..."

"To whom, child? Must we add stuttering to an already growing number of abominable peculiarities?"

"Monsieur Pinetti's g-grandfather..." she offered weakly. It sounded silly spoken aloud.

"What has the magician's grandfather to do with your unbearable burden?" The sharp tone did nothing but provoke further fretfulness that sent the drapes billowing in another, larger upsurge, an event that propelled Maman past her breaking point.

She pulled up abruptly causing Essie to stumble with the unexpected halt. Maman gripped her arm with the menace of a medieval torture device, spinning Essie to face her. Perhaps she could advise Sir Arnald on an apparatus excruciating enough to rival The Rack. On the positive side, the pain had Essie squeezing back tears, thus gaining control of her battering flurry.

"Stay clear of the nice magician, *ma chère*. I shall not have my daughter forced to marry the equivalent of an *actor*. Heed my words."

Essie supposed this was not the time to point out Monsieur Pinetti wasn't just a magician. Word was he held the title of viscount too as the son of an Earl. Not that she could choke the words past her clogged throat. How did Maman appear so calm in such fury?

Essie somehow forced herself to remain detached through the torment, for certainly she would sport a bruising rainbow of colors on the morrow. Barely nodding, so Maman could see she indeed understood, she blinked back tears while her arm pulsated with an agonizing throb.

79

The fierce grip relinquished with the same suddenness it had been obtained. "*Bien*," she smiled as if she hadn't just threatened Essie's life. "I have grand plans for you, my darling. You must not do anything stupid."

"Grand plans, Maman?" The question emerged before she could recall it. She spoke softly though.

Her large hand patted Essie's cheek. It wasn't hard but she flinched, regardless. "No need to worry your pretty head about such matters. Needless to say, your Maman has nothing but securing your most advantageous future in mind." Her hand moved to Essie's, still patting as if she were a prized poodle left with only the formality of whatever nefarious scheme she hatched in that mad brain of hers.

The urge to escape began to asphyxiate her. Yet she dare not let on.

To her relief, Maman appeared satisfied with her non-verbal reply. "Run along, darling. Remember what I said regarding the magician. I might suggest the same concerns for the Visconte Alessandro de Lecce."

That was a surprise. Whatever could Maman have against the Conte's elder son? Then resentment ripped through her, knowing *that* course should not pose a problem, but it was irritating just the same. "Is there someone more advantageous, Maman?"

"Of course, *ma chère*. But I shall take care of everything, as I always do."

A rather vague response, but an escape was an escape, and Essie grasped it. Shaking to her core, Essie felt violated. There would be no comfort in her chamber, so she ran for her other refuge, the soothing hues of hers and her sisters' private sitting room.

She was virtually guaranteed privacy with Cinde and the future king occupied with the Spanish prince, and Arnald seeing after Cill.

Tears spilled over her cheeks. How disconcerting to know no one waited to assuage her fears or felt inclined to warm her cold fingers. The life of a spinster aunt, albeit a *favorite* aunt, left her with visions of very long nights.

Essie reached the door of the out of the way chamber and checked the corridor behind her before entering. Her arm throbbed from Maman's violent fit. She went to a looking glass in the corner and straightened her soft yellow frock. Harsh, dark red fingerprints were singularly defined on her upper arm, just beneath the capped sleeve of her gown.

More tears filled her eyes, the sense of hopelessness grew overwhelming. Who could Maman possibly have in mind for her? And bless the poor fool who'd have Maman for family. What sad desperate circumstances he must find himself in, if he had to marry a woman whose eyes flutter so incessantly.

Essie pulled a lace handkerchief from her pocket, dabbed away her tears, and straightened her spine. Perhaps she was approaching the prospect wrong. Whoever he was, she could at least look forward to children in her future. She closed her eyes against her reflection. How difficult could it be to marry someone for security?

But thoughts of velvety firm lips touching hers filled her mind. Strong arms about her shoulders keeping her safe. *But he deserves better. As do I.*

"Essie?"

Essie started at the concern coming from Cinde. "Are you all right, *ma chère*?

"O-of course." She quickly swiped away the rest of her tears and spun quickly. "How did your visit go with Prince Reynardo and Princess Inez?" she asked Cinde.

Cinde grimaced. "Somewhat tedious I fear. For me more than Prince. I fear I don't speak their language well enough to understand of all that was said. But Inez is lovely. We are to meet with them again early tomorrow. Prince insists I come along, because Reynardo worries she is too shy and would be lonely." She lowered her voice. "Besides, I happen to think she may be quite far along in her lying in."

"Lying in?" Essie asked. "She's with child? But the travel..."

Cinde's hand fluttered in the air. "She is not so far along that she is showing. Truly, having a child is natural business. I foresee no problem in her visit." She shrugged.

Ha! Cinde's insistence in having a child as "natural business" was all well and good, but Cinde had almost perished with Edric. The memory sent a shudder up Essie's spine.

"Whose visit is a problem?" Cill said coming through the door.

"Princess Inez, and her visit is *not* a problem," Cinde told her. "And as the coronation festivities are so finely planned, I am not so missed."

"Wait until you hear what you did miss!" Essie said. "We were playing Charades, which I handily won—and Cill here insisted on quite another show—" Cill grabbed her arm; pressing on the already forming discoloration Maman had generously gifted her.

"—Hmm, you under estimate yourself greatly, *ma chère,*" Cill said to Cinde.

"I fear I shall be wearing long sleeves for the coronation ceremony." Essie muttered, scowling at Cill who returned a pointed look.

Cill let go quickly, and demanded. "What happened to your arm?"

"Maman paid me a visit. I came here to hide."

Cill turned to Cinde and frowned. "Cinde, I hesitate to say this but 'tis becoming critical we do something about Maman. Her current behavior cannot continue. I fear she might hurt someone. 'Tis only a matter of time."

It took a moment for Cill's silent message to finally register in Essie's slowed thoughts. The painful throb in her arm had eliminated her ability to think coherently.

"*Oui,* but I am torn in how to handle the matter. Papa loved her. Therein lays my dilemma. Why else would he have married her?"

Essie lifted her head at this and exchanged a surprised glance with Cill. "Oh, dear," she said.

"I am not sure, Cinde." Cill shrugged. "But 'twas not a love match. Most likely lands." Cill let out a sigh and dropped into an overstuffed chair.

Essie forgot her pained arm and noted Cill's wan cheeks with concern.

"I-I don't understand," Cinde frowned.

"The marriage probably had naught to do with love. I fear your fairy godmother placed notions that with love comes marriage in that idealistic nature of yours," Cill said. "Yours was a fairy tale of monumental proportions. One that will, no doubt, be told through the ages of time."

"There is no need for condescension," Cinde said, sharply.

"She meant nothing of the sort and you know it," Essie said. "After all, Cill is more than happily married to Arnald, *oui*? I am the one left with no hope of such a future." Essie failed to keep the bitterness from her tone as Alessandro's declarations to the

Conte rushed her memory. And with Maman's latest demands on *not* engaging his affections—

"I have every faith that your Visconte Alessandro de Lecce will come through as a shining hero," Cinde said smiling, faith obviously restored.

"You and his father, perhaps," she muttered. But she'd rather live in the stews of London than hand him her heart now. Pain squeezed her chest in a curdled grip.

"Your feelings can't have changed that drastically, Essie," Cill accused through closed eyes.

"Why not? He seems bent on Lady Kendra, besides," she said mildly. "That blond ninny been attached to his side since my rendition of 'The Shrew' this afternoon." She glanced quickly at Cill, suddenly understanding the blunt, yet effective, change in conversation topic. Cill didn't want to frighten Cinde. Essie wanted to bang her head against the wall at her self-centeredness. What had she been thinking?

"What was it you overheard?" Cinde asked gently.

The concern from her sisters on the cusp of Maman's confrontation was too much. And once again tears blurred her vision. They spilt forth like the rushing break in a dam, her sobs filling the private chamber. But pride still refused to let Alessandro's condemning words to the Conte squeeze past her lips, even when Cinde's arms encompassed her in a fierce hug.

Pulling herself together, Essie stepped back and smiled through a watery gaze. "My apologies. I fear I am more distraught over the discord with Maman than I first believed. I shall be fine. I...I promise you." She took a last sniff and a measured breath, restoring her composure, if somewhat tentative.

Cill rose. "Mayhap we could all use a breath of air," she said going to the door. "I vow this feeling of unending nausea would fell even the strongest of stern constitutions. I don't understand it. 'Tis most annoying."

Acute lightness settled over Essie. She was blessed. After all, she had her niece and nephew, and her beloved sisters. She followed the latter two to the corridor grinning. "I suppose I could attempt to give the night breeze some heightened speed," she offered with an attempt at humor. One had to be realistic about these things.

Cinde stepped forward and linked an arm through Cill's while Essie sidled up on Cill's other side. They meandered their way to large glass doors at the corridor's end where bright moonlight lit the hall from the evening sky. It was so clean and clear, Essie could make out the ripples in the pond surrounding the statue of Eros.

Muted harmony filled Essie as the three of them stepped on the terrace into the crisp night air. The fragrance of maturing spices scented the air, clearing Essie's head and the last of her melancholy state. She was a fool to let that *imbecilé's* asinine comments hurt her so. Eye-affliction notwithstanding, she had much to offer. Aside from being sister to the princess-soon-to-be-queen, she was quite brilliant in her own right. She was a wizard with numbers. She loved children. She had dainty feet...

But Maman's harsh warning pierced left Essie floundering for more answers to unasked questions—like whom she planned on Essie wedding. Nothing made sense.

"What is Alessandro de Lecce doing out here? And why is he whispering with Monsieur Pinetti?" Cinde asked. Essie followed her gaze to the far side of the pond where indeed Alessandro and the magician seemed to be engaged in heated discussion, tones hushed.

"I can't hear a thing," Cill whispered. Apparently, the crisp night air agreed with her, her spirits quite revived.

"We would not want to be caught eavesdropping," Essie said dryly.

"Well, of course not, silly." Cill clung to her and Cinde's arms and ran.

It was an effective move, Essie realized, tugging them to the edging forest.

Essie froze. Indeed, as did her sisters. By unspoken agreement none of the three dared move, thus revealing their hidden spot among the trees. Cill was right: one should never eavesdrop. Leastways with one's sisters.

Alessandro's voice rang loudly in the stilled darkness. "That was quite the show you bestowed upon us this afternoon, Joseph. I was suitably impressed. I see your technique improves. Not to mention lucky as the prince's cousin did not see fit to have you caned or tossed below."

Essie heard Cinde's sharp gasp and saw Cill squeeze her hand.

"Yes, and I suppose it's you I have you to thank for saving my sorry arse."

"Sorry, old man. It wasn't me. I was too late."

"Then who—" Monsieur Pinetti sounded genuinely surprised.

"I hear that Lady Esmeralda was asking questions. Personally I would have enlightened them on some of your most guarded secrets, and had them lock you up and throw away the key. As luck would have it—*yours*—and your guileless surprise turned out to be your saving grace. Besides I was not the only one to see you speaking to that young boy."

A short awkward silence filled the air before Alessandro's tone took on a renewed attack. "What in blasted hell were you thinking, pulling a stunt like that?"

"What are you talking about?"

"I see you still hone in on the lone female in company, *no*?" The derision in Alessandro's voice cut Essie deep. She understood his message well enough. If *he* had no interest in her, what reason should another? White hot anger blurred her vision that had her blinking back furious tears. The blood that surged through her veins in a rush of vehement furor showed in the trees, denoted by a deluged cluster of falling leaves.

"I fail to see your interest in the matter, de Lecce. You were more than occupied, as I recall." Monsieur Pinetti laughed then. The sound sent a shiver crawling up Essie's spine. "We have run into this sort of competition before, *non*? I am surprised you need reminding."

"I don't require a reminder," Alessandro bit out.

Essie's palm flew to her mouth, stifling her gasp. She was *competition?* Fulminating rants were held back only by the hand she kept in place.

The whole exchange was confusing, infuriating.

"*Merci*, my friend. 'Tis always a pleasure to impress the opposition."

Friend? Competition? Oh, now she was beyond furious. With compressed lips she squeezed her hands into fists, breaking a fingernail, in her ire. She'd show that—that—*blackguard.* She started to rise.

Cill grasped her arm—right on her newly forming bruise. Essie bit back the pain—the physical *and* the one shattering her already depressed and ebbing confidence.

Tense silence followed Monsieur Pinetti's odd statement. Obviously, the two shared more history than anyone suspected.

"Is this what your cryptic note was meant to do? Stir up old rivalries?"

Essie would have sold her soul for a peek. Mayhap if she shifted just slightly—a whisper rumbled through the trees. Cill shot her a pointed glare.

An unnatural silence escalated between the two men. She froze, waiting for the moment they stumbled upon them—accusations screaming.

Then guilt settled over her at their precarious position. She deserved to rot in a rat-infested dungeon placing her sisters in such. For Cinde, the soon-to-be queen, caught hiding in the trees like a truant schoolboy. Why it would serve to embarrass, not just Cinde, but her prince, his maman—their kingdom. All Cinde held dear.

An awkward hush mounted between Monsieur Pinetti and Alessandro. Essie waited in suspended agony. The fluctuating whisper through the trees had her squeezing her eyes tight, not daring to breathe.

THE WIND WAS A dead giveaway. The meddling little chit was in the area, but Aless would deal with *her* later. He lowered his voice and hissed, choosing his words carefully. "Do not toy with her affections, Joseph. I will not hesitate to call you out."

Joseph tilted his head seeming to listen to the night. Crickets chirped, frogs croaked, leaves rustled. But it was the sudden drop in breeze, the finally constant norm that allowed Aless a cautious breath. He hoped Joseph had not caught onto Lady Esmeralda's little specialty.

Joseph pierced him with the mesmerists' eyes for which he was becoming so well known. "Call me out? We both know I am the better shot, my friend."

"That would be determined." Aless prayed Lady Esmeralda remained hidden deep enough in the woods, unable to make out their words. She would not find their direction so flattering.

Joseph leaned in and smacked his lips as if he'd just sampled a particularly luscious dessert. "She is a morsel, no? Quite...*desirable*." His slight hesitation was deliberate.

Sucking in a measured breath, Aless reminded himself his friend was an expert at goading him. They understood each other too well.

"Besides, you know better than most I am not the wastrel society believes."

Aless pushed a hand through already wind-ruffled hair. "*Sì,*" he agreed, though he loathed admitting it.

"Whether my grandfather chooses to acknowledge the fact or not, my father lives—titled nobility in the heart of Yorkshire." He lowered his voice to match Alessandro's. "She could do much worse than me, my friend."

It was true. And the thought did not sit well. Alessandro had a sudden urge to plow a fist into Joseph elegant looking nose.

Straightening suddenly, Joseph turned serious. "Let us walk. I have information you may deem vital. Something disturbs the atmosphere here."

Alessandro rolled his eyes skyward. He had no idea. After a quick perusal about, Alessandro followed Joseph toward the outer perimeter of the lawns, a half-moon lighting their path.

They walked for a time before Joseph stopped and faced Alessandro. "There is talk of a siege."

"Don't be ridiculous," Aless snapped. But the fingers of dread lifted the hair off his nape. The Conte's words slammed through him, recanting his father's odd behavior of late. "Who has power to stage a siege?"

"I believe 'tis your *padre*, my friend."

Alessandro's fist shot out before common sense could prevail, his reaction perfunctory. Too bad, he'd missed Joseph's nose.

"You shall pay for that," Joseph told him rubbing his jaw, lips twitching. "But, I shall forgive your lack of restraint. 'Tis obvious my words have caused you undue distress."

Alessandro shook out his fist, knuckles throbbing. "How dare you imply such a farce?"

"The evidence suggests differently," Joseph said quietly.

"What evidence?"

A pained expression crossed Joseph's face.

"No evidence, then," Aless confirmed.

"Granted. No *solid* evidence. 'Tis more a vision. Regardless..." Joseph tugged something from his pocket and held out an open palm. Glittering diamonds winked in the moonlight on a delicate band of silver.

Aless hissed. "Are you thieving now?" Joseph ignored him, but it mattered naught when it began to dawn on Aless what he was seeing. "Are those *diamonds*?"

"*Certainement.* 'Tis a spectacular piece of jewelry, *non*?" With an unusual sense of urgency, Joseph pressed it into his hand. "I give this to you in friendship. It warrants special powers. But I advise you to use it wisely."

Aless studied the bracelet closely, unease still tingling the base of his scalp. A dragon creature with emeralds filling its slanted eyes, so dark in their depths, they appeared black—reminiscent of a certain copper-haired miss. Rubies formed a path of breathing fire that would encircle only the frailest of wrists. Priceless. "What mean you, 'special powers'? And what need have I of something so small?" he frowned. "I don't understand."

Joseph lowered his voice. "The wearer becomes invisible to the naked eye. 'Tis my visions that say you shall need it more than me. Fair warning, my friend." He turned and walked away.

Heat singed Aless's palm where the brilliant wristlet rested. He would be a fool to ignore Joseph's portend. After all, they'd served in the war together and no one knew better than he that while Joseph's predictions were haphazard at best, the few that managed to come to pass were unerringly acute.

Chapter 14

"OH, MY," CILL SAID.

The breathless wonder in her voice made Essie certain she was teasing her in a cruel jest. Essie sat on the ground hidden among the trees, stunned by the exchange they'd overheard.

"*Oui.*" Cinde's had the same airy quality.

Hands fisted at her sides, shoulders drawn, Essie swallowed back more forthcoming tears. "So now you both know," she rasped. The tears obscured her vision.

"Know what?" Cinde asked. Confusion marred her features, not that the moonlight was any help. "It sounded to me as if the Visconte de Lecce felt it necessary to call out his friend—if Monsieur Pinetti even hinted at treating you without respect."

"*Mais oui,* 'twas the same impression I received," Cill said.

"Hah! Monsieur Pinetti was just using me to entice Lady Kendra's affections. Don't you see? That is where Signore de Lecce's attentions were." The tears spilled over onto her cheeks.

"Ridiculous." Cinde, the ultimate optimist and believer in happily-ever-afters, smiled and patted her hand.

Essie was so angry, some of the animosity from their younger days broiled just below the surface. But she clenched her jaw keep any hurtful accusations from bursting out.

"I vow they find you undeniably attractive. Both of them."

"There is more to it than you know," Essie bit out softly. Difficult, through grinding teeth.

"Like what?" Cinde said gently. Essie was hardly aware that Cinde had grasped her hand.

"The Conte told Alessandro 'twas time for him to marry." She sucked in a deep breath. "That...that I was as good a choice as any."

"You are," Cinde assured her, squeezing her hand.

"You failed to let me finish. The Visconte you are so quick to defend stated he would not marry a woman who could change the weather on a whim." Despondency gripped her by the throat. She jerked her hand from Cinde's and shoved the tears away, furious they dared fall over such a blackguard.

"Oh, my," Cill said. "I can see where you might be a bit discouraged in your affections."

"My *affections*? Aptly put." Essie stood and shook out her skirts.

Cinde came to her feet as well. Cill, apparently, did not seem in any such hurry.

"It sounded to me as if Alessandro de Lecce and Viscount Lawrie, Chevalier Joseph Pinetti were fighting over some *lone* miss. And that lone miss could only be you," Cinde said, gently.

"Bah! Even were that the case, there are still Maman's threats from earlier," she frowned.

"There is that," Cill said. Her voice sounded weary. Concerned, Essie glanced at her.

"What was that nonsense about Edric?" Cinde asked.

Essie caught Cill's silent message and agreed. It would only worry Cinde, what with all the strangers milling about the castle and grounds. She shook off her dole misgivings and handed them a wry smile. "I appreciate your confidence in my flirtatious abilities," she told them, blatantly ignoring Cinde's question.

"'Tis certainly enlightening." A light mischievousness fell over her. "I am surprised at the two of you. It seems you are missing the advantages of the long-term scenario."

"And what is that, *ma chère*?" Cinde asked.

"As the favorite spinster aunt I shall always be around for your children."

"I think I am going to be sick," Cill said thickly. She turned her head and cast up accounts several meters away.

ALESSANDRO WATCHED JOSEPH'S retreating figure in a bit of a stunned stupor. His implications were dire. Still, Aless denied what his heart told him was true. That Padre had truly lost his mind. Simmering rage tempered by fear hovered just below the surface.

What purpose would Joseph have in lying? Had Alessandro missed signs of his father's madness? The answer to that was easy enough. While Aless had been at war the past couple of years, his father had been plotting to take over Chalmers. 'Twas inconceivable. But if Joseph was correct in his premonitions, his father must be stopped. Nothing but danger stood in his current path.

Aless heaved in a deep breath. First and foremost, was to find some way to control his father's unmanageable tongue. But how? To keep the Conte from spilling such sentiments aloud would require instilling a quick and successful plan. It was beyond possible that they leave before the coronation ceremony. Their absence would be construed as suspicious. Aless pushed a hand through his hair again and cast a surreptitious glance about. The sudden wind had dissipated. Mayhap, Lady Esmeralda had made good her escape back to the castle. He supposed he'd best do the same before someone realized he'd gone missing.

"Good evening, my lord."

The gruff voice startled him. He turned and bit back a growl. Lady Esmeralda's mother was a sight to behold—one of terror. How much had she heard? "Lady Roche, 'tis cool this evening. And here you are without your wrap. Might I escort you to the ballroom?"

She latched onto him with surprising strength. Though considering her massive girth—

"I was unaware that you and Monsieur Pinetti were such grand acquaintances. 'Tis quite the secret the two of you hold." Her heartwarming chuckle failed to cover her attempted guile. That answered that question; she'd heard correctly. How was he to deny her accusation now?

"*Sí, Signora.* We were actually in school together."

"His father is an earl?

"Indeed. Joseph holds a title of his own, Viscount Lawrie."

"How very interesting, *oui*? He finds my Esmeralda endearing, I daresay." They walked much slower than he preferred. The doors to the terrace might well be in Spain.

He cringed. She'd heard plenty. "*Sí.* That is so."

"I see you watching my sweet, Esmeralda, as well, *non*?" Her tone slipped into something more menacing.

He forced himself to continue his nonchalant pace. "Watching, *Signora*? She is most attractive." He chuckled. "I like to think she and I are friends. After all, I have known her since she was betrothed to Prince Charming, *sí*?"

Her grip tightened, demonstrating her displeasure. He flexed the muscle. Such intimidation was useless against him. War was fraught with greater hazards. To best him, she'd need a far more menacing tenure.

"Ah, but her unfortunate eye affliction—" She shook her head, as if *he* believed her simulated sympathy. "—such a deterrent, eh?"

It sounded almost as if she were discouraging his attentions. It took a moment before his confusion shifted to outrage. They'd reached the terrace steps. He stopped and offered her a benign curl of the lips. "I believe her eye affliction is not the deterrent you fear, Madame."

She dropped her hold as if the bracelet in his pocket had fire flickering through his skin, through the sleeve of his coat. Evil seared those robust features, the glare in her eye, ominous. "'Tis obvious I am not making myself understood." Her tone turned low, scathing. "You shall stay clear of my daughter, *Signore*, or I shall make certain my son-in-law, the prince, learns of a certain impending plot." With that she spun and disappeared through the smattering of couples.

"*Touché,* Madame," he said to her retreated figure. How dare she! How dare she imply her daughter ineligible for his affection due to some small nervous misfortune not of her own making! The second the thoughts were formed he realized how true they rang.

Aless groaned. But hadn't he implied that very ideal to the Conte just days before? Worse yet, Lady Esmeralda had heard his damaging remarks, personally, and would now ne'er believe those were not his true feelings.

His irritation with the Conte's demands overrode his sensitivity. But that was just an excuse, and a weak one at that. It was difficult admitting he held deep regard for Lady Esmeralda, and had for some time. He thought about the war he'd returned from, other friends he'd known, some he'd lost. Many were known to have turned on the women they esteemed in the worst possible way. Might he not be any different? But flashing green eyes filling his inner vision convinced him he was much different.

He shook off the angst. This was no time to dwell on such matters. Now, more than ever, he must stop whatever plans the Conte seem to have in place. Regardless, Madame Hilda's threats fell on deaf ears. He had plans for her lovely daughter.

Aless started forward but remembered Lady Esmeralda's tendency towards eavesdropping and turned back. A small smile eased the tightness in his chest. The webbed trees were surrounded in an ominous dark. Surprise touched him when he saw her *and* her sisters skirting the Eros pond. He kept a watchful eye until they disappeared safely within the confines of the castle.

He found himself reluctant to give up the crisp night air and the soft sconce lighting, but duty called. Chalmers had surely never belonged to the de Lecces. The idea was ludicrous, *wasn't it*? Aless worked his way up the steps, letting out a sigh. Like it or not the time had come for confrontation.

The ballroom held a majority of guests recently arrived. A small orchestra played wind instruments, oblivious to any overhanging threat. The room offered no appeal with its stuffy air and political pretenses. And despite his inner turmoil Aless searched the room, carefully keeping his expression blank. To no avail. Was there no one in whom he could confide, anyone to quell the beliefs proving his father wrong. Joseph? Sabato? Niccòlo?

He rounded the corner.

"Ooh—" the feminine cry startled him.

Both hands landed on pale arms to steady her. "My pardon, Lady Kendra. Are you quite all right?"

"Yes. Yes, of course." She spoke with just enough flirtatious breathy demure, fluttering lashes, and wide-eyed innocence to appear uncontrived. He just managed to hide a wince.

"Thank you." She clamped onto him with undue possession. Not unlike that of Lady Roche. Perhaps not as staunched, but braced just the same. Thankfully, the walk was short. Unfortunately, not short enough.

"'Tis dancing, milord," she said gaily.

"Is there?" He sounded like an idiot. But how to put her off? He guided her through the ballroom carefully skirting the dance floor as an idea came to him. "How did you enjoy Pinetti's performance, Lady Kendra?"

"'Twas somewhat eerie, in truth." A delicate shudder touched her shoulders. "But I am familiar with his *stage* work." Her disgust was poignant.

Aless smiled. "Viscount Lawrie is a friend of mine from years past," he informed her. "Punch?" Alessandro snatched up a glass. Padre was up to his tricks, it would seem.

"But—"

He thrust it in her hand.

She turned wide, adoring eyes on him. "Thank you," she said softly.

"I wonder what brought him to Chalmers." Aless said this more to himself.

Her eyes strayed to the dance floor where Joseph was making his bows to a matronly partner. "I believe his maternal grandfather lives in the vicinity. My father said his father despises the French side of his lineage," she said.

"He's a good man," Aless said harshly.

She gasped.

"My apologies, Lady Kendra. We served in the war together. I would stand by friend no matter the circumstances."

The elderly matron blushed at something Joseph whispered to her. The man was egregious. He glanced up and caught Aless and Lady Kendra watching. Aless acknowledged him with a silent salute. Joseph grinned and switched his gaze to Lady Kendra and winked. Her lips compressed.

"I see you are not as enamored of my friend as are most of the other persons of female persuasion, *Signorina*. Impressive." His respect for her intelligence raised another notch. She, at least, showed some sense when it came to the opposite sex. Joseph could charm a cobra.

She snorted drawing a startled glance. It was soft, but definitely a snort.

A hum rippled through the crowd. Surprise jarred him when Lady Esmeralda appeared in the archway with a pale Lady Pricilla. Yet he saw no sign of the princess.

There was a new set to Lady Esmeralda's jaw Aless hadn't noticed before. Flushed cheeks, hair just out of sorts—nothing overt, of course, just a tad...*windblown*. He was almost certain no one else noticed. One other thing out of place was the elbow-length gloves she'd donned. They caught his eye only because Lady Pricilla's hands were bare.

She and Lady Pricilla edged their way towards the refreshments but were intercepted by Sir Arnald. Aless scanned the crowd for Lady Roche but she'd not yet returned. With Lady Kendra still stuck to his side, he managed to maneuver his way into Lady Esmeralda's path—quite nicely, by his estimation. She pulled up to an abrupt halt.

"Good evening, Madame," Lady Kendra said in perfect demure respect. Lady Esmeralda's flinch was as subtle as Lady Kendra's insult.

"*Signorina.*" Alessandro hoped his address would smooth the moment over. He had a moment of regret for landing Lady Esmeralda in this position.

The brilliance of her green eyes still unnerved him, and he strove to elongate the greeting. "Have you been allowed to enjoy the evening air?" he asked. Panic flared in her eyes and she spun away quickly. She bumped into Joseph.

"Lady Esmeralda, how enchanting you look." Joseph bowed. "Mayhap you would favor me with this dance?" His smooth tones set Alessandro's teeth grinding so hard it was a wonder they didn't crumble under the stress.

Aless stepped forward, but Lady Kendra's hand was like a vice.

"Would you see me to my papa, *Signore* de Lecce? I fear he will wonder what has become of me." That breathy rush was beginning to annoy him.

"Of course, *Signorina.*" Not that he had any choice. "Please excuse us, Lady Esmeralda, Joseph." He clicked his heels. For naught, as it was to their retreating forms.

But not before he caught the tale-tell sign of a surging updraft in the atmosphere.

Damnation!

"How was the night air, milady?"

"T-the n-night air?" Essie knew it was rude to close her eyes, but what alternative had she to still the sudden flutters? Monsieur Pinetti's voice was soft like butter under the heat of a spring day, his touch at her waist, light. She prayed Maman was anywhere but the ballroom.

"Come now, do not tell me you were not in the vicinity outdoors when I met with my friend Alessandro just moments ago."

She swallowed and knew he'd heard it.

"I fear your..." He hesitated before saying, gently, "...*condition* gives you away, you know."

Fury gripped her. She flashed her eyes at him and stopped. It failed to matter as his hold firmed and he swept her into lavish spin. With effort she reined in her temper. The arrogant blackguard. She'd show him. "Condition?" she asked sweetly, turning a brilliant all-teeth smile on him.

Surprise colored his features, and he stumbled. Oh, not that anyone but she noticed, considering how quickly he recovered. Still, irritation flared through her at his obvious skill. But then, to her disgust, he had the unmitigated gall to...to *laugh*. Well, not very loud, she signified but the restraint was obvious.

"Lady Esmeralda, it would be remiss of me to not mention to you how striking a figure you are in a temper. All fire and...well, ahem. Mayhap, I should just leave it at that."

Confused, she narrowed her eyes on him. "Fire? Why, sir, it sounds almost as if you compliment me."

He inclined his head. "For certain, milady." He swung her to a slow stop. "The music has ended," he said softly.

Chapter 15

DELIVERING LADY KENDRA TO the Earl of Macclesfield was much like loosening a garret from Alessandro's neck. It was not gone, only offering less restrictive relief that threatened to tighten again at any given moment.

The earl eyed him as he might a stud stallion he was considering for purchase to sire his future breed. Aless resisted the urge to tug at the noose...er...cravat circumventing his collar. He pulled himself up to his full height and eyed the earl, refusing to back away like a trapped animal. The earl turned to his daughter and said something Aless had already lost interest in.

He glanced about the ballroom, surprised by the number of guests that seemed to grow by the moment. When he caught sight of Lady Esmeralda, he did not know whether to be relieved or alarmed by the vision of radiating anger, palpable by the shards of chipped emeralds firing from those brilliant eyes. He found it bewildering, trying to reconcile the sight before him now compared to her usual nervous fluttering. It heightened his urgency in retrieving her from his friend. But then he almost laughed outright when the usually unflappable, man-about-town, Joseph, stumbled through the waltz. He straightened quickly enough, but Aless savored the moment nonetheless.

What a sight she was to behold, that blaze flashing—until the exact moment Aless witnessed his friend's stunned realization—that of her true inner beauty. Devil take it! He fisted a hand, fighting for composure. Stampeding the dance floor would not endear him to the royal family; nor would creating a scene with Lady Esmeralda.

The need for air overtook him and he excused himself from Lady Kendra and the earl, and hastened his way to the French doors. A brisk walk would surely keep him from following through on his threat in calling out his old friend.

Aless was puzzled by the understated change in Lady Esmeralda. It was something he couldn't quite define. And why the sudden transformation in sentiment should bother him so, he could not fathom. Mayhap it was the trace of tears and the proud tilt of her head when she'd boldly faced him moments after his grand *faux pas*. Or the tiny arms of a small child wrapped about her neck declaring the solidity of his love. Or, perhaps it came in the startling knowledge he'd witnessed in the cutting shards of those glittering green eyes. Aless managed to wind his way onto the terrace without further interruption.

Si. There was much more to Lady Esmeralda than her cursed blight. Placing his hands flat atop the stone wall at waist height, he looked out into the dark night and inhaled deeply. For the first time he wondered at the anguish she must endure when certain events caught her unawares.

"Visconte de Lecce?" He froze at the formal use of his title. Something he'd not heard since he'd been abroad.

Aless swiveled to her voice in the dark. "Lady Pricilla. I see you crave the crisp air as well, *no*?"

A soft shudder rippled touched her shoulders, startling him. "*Certainement*, I can scarce stand *not* to breathe the crisp air, for some ungodly reason."

"You are not well?"

103

She narrowed her gaze on him. 'Twas quite severe in the soft lighting on the terrace. "Bah! I do not wish to speak of me, my lord. 'Tis my sister I am here to discuss."

"*MON...DIEU*," ESSIE BREATHED, trying to make her escape from Monsieur Pinetti. His hold was...was *most* inappropriate...and *laughing* at her *condition?* What nerve. Why, she'd turn him into a toad if she had hold of that little silver baton she and her sisters had had possession of some four years prior.

"Might I offer you some refreshment, Lady Esmeralda?" Monsieur Pinetti asked. She gave him a bright smile, knowing full well it was false.

"*Merci beaucoup,* that would be lovely." Essie only felt the slightest twinge of guilt when he bowed and strode for the punch before making good her escape through the throngs of couples. Each and every one sucked the very oxygen from the ballroom. It appeared a good majority of the guests for the coronation ceremony had suddenly arrived.

Cinde stood off to one side on Prince's arm, cornered by the Earl of Macclesfield and Lady Kendra. Essie refused to acknowledge her relief that Alessandro was nowhere to be seen in the vicinity of the little she-cat. Madame, indeed.

Maman finally appeared and had the Conte trapped on a settee with no chance for flight. Swallowing a relieved chuckle, Essie made her way out by ducking behind several potted plants.

The ballroom did not appear large enough for all the puffy skirts and high collars. Blessedly, the terrace doors stood wide. That is where she would find Cill. Her wan features of late would have her choking for air.

"I do not wish to speak about me, my lord," she heard Cill say as she stepped through the doors. "'Tis my sister I would like to discuss."

"Cill," Essie hissed, startling her. *Bien!* She deserved nothing less. "I believe I can speak for myself."

Cill paused, seeming to consider her words. Then with a deliberate pause and scathing glance at Alessandro, Cill nodded. "I'm sure you can. My apologies, Essie. If you'll excuse me, *Signore*?"

"Of course, milady," Alessandro said mildly. The silence turned awkward once Cill disappeared back inside.

Alessandro turned to Essie. The blanket of night hid the details of his expression, but she could make out the sharp angles of his cheeks, his jaw. His voice was liquid velvet, luring her like a steel trap. "It appears Lady Pricilla happened onto my blundered words."

Heat flooded Essie's cheeks. Thankfully, she was certain he couldn't see any better than she. Rather than admitting anything, Essie said, "I see you have let the jewel you escorted escape your clutches." Her petulant tone had her masking a wince. She concluded with a sharp tone, "You best be careful, *Signore*, or Monsieur Pinetti is likely to whisk Lady Kendra from under your nose." *Your strong aquiline nose.*

The click of his heels sounded, and the shadow of his head inclined. "Touché, Lady Esmeralda." She did not need to see the curve of his lips since the amusement resounding against the stone in the enshrouded-fogged air that cocooned them. The intimacy startled her. "Perhaps it is you who seeks my friend, Joseph?"

"Of all—"

He overrode her protests by snagging her arm and leading her down the steps into the low lit gardens. "Come, let's walk."

She gasped when his grip firmed on Maman's generously bestowed gift, leaving no doubt of his determination.

His hand loosened and he spun, blocking her path, so quickly she stumbled into him. "What is it?" he demanded.

If she weren't so angry, she'd almost swear concern marred his features, but then it was dark.

"You're hurt?"

Through gritted teeth, Essie bit out, "Visconte de Lecce, *s'il vous plaît*."

She heard the hitch in his voice. "Why the sudden formality, Lady Esmeralda?" She caught the gleam of a wicked smile, barely discernible, in the soft lighting.

Mayhap two could play at this game. She graced him the same smile she'd turned on Monsieur Pinetti, fixating on her earlier ire. "'Tis an excellent question, my lord. *Alessandro*." Unfortunately, his name came out on a much huskier note than she'd intended, closer to a whisper.

He stilled, and she swallowed.

Clasping her gloved hand, he placed it on his arm, quite properly so, and continued down the path in a leisurely trek.

Soft, dewy fog hovered, dampening the glowing embers from the torches lining the path, and soft hushed voices hummed. A few minutes later Alessandro pulled her up before a painted gazebo. Only yesterday she would gladly have died for such a moment with him. But, that was before she'd learned his true feelings.

Essie speared him with a narrow gaze. Why drag her out here, then? What nefarious scheme had he up his well fitted sleeve? She clenched her fist and tried to pull away but he held tight.

Fortunately, Cill was not Prince's only student of self-defense. Her sister had managed an admirable job four years ago having been kidnapped by a smuggler. By the time Sir Arnald had burst in to rescue her she'd flattened the villain out, knocking him dead. Of course, Essie had no desire to kill Alessandro de Lecce; but maiming him a bit would suffice. In a swift maneuver, she swiped a hairpin where a curl tumbled across her forehead and poked his hand.

His hand jerked from her arm, his startled expression, beyond price.

"I would be very cautious, were I you, my lord. If you are discovered here with me, you may find yourself bound for life to a woman whose eyes could—" she tapped an index finger against her chin. "Let me see how well my memory serves—'flutter so furiously 'tis enough to create an avalanche in these Pyrenees Mountains'. *Oui.* I believe I have it rightly so."

He rubbed the back of his hand, and she experienced, then squelched a plague of doubt for her unladylike comportment. "Any doubts I had on your listening and retaining abilities have been assuaged. *Grazie, Signorina.*"

She found herself blinking back unexpected tears. "You're welcome, sir." She spun, desperate to make an escape back up the path. But found herself once again stayed by that unrelenting grip.

He slid his hand down to hers, confiscating the hairpin. As gently as he pleased, he pinned the wayward curl back into place. "I have no designs on Lady Kendra," he told her.

"I don't recall asking if you did," she retorted. Again, irritatingly breathless.

"Regardless, I wanted you to know." His voice dropped lower, sending the butterflies in her stomach into chaos. And—oh, no. The wind picked up in velocity. Essie squeezed her eyes shut.

Tight.

'Twas then she felt the heat of his breath seconds before the soft pressure of his lips captured hers in her very first kiss. It was nothing, and everything, she'd dreamed. Firm and soft, his lips were like rich velvet. They moved tentatively over hers as if he feared he would scare her away. But she'd waited *five long years* for this one moment. She found she did not *want* to run, much to her disgust. The most delightful of sensations tumbled through her. Her hands found their way flat against his chest, and started creeping up. She wanted to savor, experience, luxuriate in—

'tis enough to create an avalanche...

The unbidden words crashed through her head, jarring her bliss. She shoved against his unmovable form causing her to stumble back. Not him.

ALESS CAUGHT LADY ESMERALDA to his chest before she could land on her backside. His heart pounded furiously; blood roared through his ears. He could feel her trembling fingers through his confusion. The breeze kicked up immensely, leaving no doubt to his affect on her. She was young, untried, terrified.

"H-how dare y-you," she sputtered.

Instead of feeling ashamed as he ought, he couldn't seem to think of anything except kissing her again. How softly her mouth conformed to his. Moonlight glistened off her damp lips, her eyes lit up the night sky. Something stark speared him. Something fitting, like home? *Sí*, Lady Esmeralda felt like home.

If they were caught it would mean...

Aless took her by the shoulders, and though tempted to kiss her again, turned her and gently pushed her back to the path from which they'd veered. He had a feeling rest would be as elusive as Lady Esmeralda's acknowledged affection.

"Sleep well, milady," he said gruffly.

Chapter 16

FRESH DEW CLUNG TO the leaves and grass the next afternoon. It was all that was left from the trace of rain the previous day. From the looks of things, the weather would not play havoc with the days scheduled activities. There was much anticipation regarding the archery tournament.

Alessandro had his sights set on tea with the family, or would have if he could have kept his mind from the onslaught of soft full lips and fluttering green eyes. A slight groan escaped and he forced himself back to matters of dire urgency like somehow maneuvering the conversation to Chalmers' beginnings.

Unfortunately, he couldn't seem to relinquish an image of copper tresses intermingled with his fingers. Of releasing pinned curls rather than stifling them. The night before, when sleep was so fitful, when he'd teetered on the edge of light slumber, his dreams were filled with the sweetest lavender and warm fingers gripping his shoulders.

Once he'd relinquished Lady Esmeralda back to the terrace, 'twas a blessing the only glance he'd met was Lady Pricilla's grim one. Lady Pricilla would be surprised to find Aless's thoughts of her sister were both carnal *and* honorable.

Hands clasped at his lower back, he struggled to recall Joseph's words—accusations, more like—and the Conte's conspicuous absence from most of the previous night's festivities. He stood and moved to the wooden box lying atop his dressing table, unlatched the brass fastening, and lifted the lid. He lifted the delicate jeweled band, savored the heat radiating from fiery rubies. He prayed it worked, if and when the time presented itself.

Aless dropped the bracelet back in the box and pulled the chain of his pocket watch and flipped it open: nine a.m. Waiting for a response from the missive he'd sent his uncle could be days, not hours, he chastised himself. He stuffed the watch back into his pocket, knowing it told him nothing except he was hungry and wasting time in his chamber when he should be in the breakfast room discovering the past. Seeing if anything the Conte told him regarding Chalmers past was remotely true. Aless pressed his lips together. It mattered naught, really. Just the Conte belief the kingdom was rightly theirs raised the stakes considerably.

The unpredictability of the situation was enough to give one heart failure. What could his father be thinking? Weren't the tentative relations between the French and Spanish strained enough? Alessandro, having spent two and a half of the past four years fighting a senseless war between the Portuguese and Italians, shuddered at this recent development.

A sharp knock pierced his thoughts.

"Enter," he barked.

"Aless?" Niccòlo leaned in.

Perfect. Just what he needed. "*Si*, Niccòlo," he sighed.

"I fear something strange is going on." It could have been a touch of fear, Aless detected, but his younger brother sounded just that, very young.

"What is it?"

Niccòlo glanced over his shoulder before crossing foot into the chamber, latching the door behind him. "There are some odd rumblings being tarried about."

This gut-clenching fear was becoming all too familiar. "Sit."

"I am not a dog," he mumbled. But he threw himself down in a wing-backed chair before the hearth.

Aless dropped into the chair opposite, and studied his brother. He rested his forearms on his thighs, hands clasped. Mayhap it was time to confess his fears to his brother.

"You seemed worried. What is it, Aless?"

Aless was surprised at the depth of Niccòlo's insight. Or perhaps Aless failed more at hiding his fear. Carefully weighing his words, he said, "I fear Padre has a notion that Chalmers Kingdom was stolen from his clutches."

Niccòlo snorted. "How is that possible? We are Italian."

"*Sí*. But he seems to believe that the...uh...theft occurred close to a century past."

"I don't understand," Niccòlo said, shaking his head. "What a ridiculous—"

"Ridiculous or not, he believes it is so." Aless grimaced. "I'm concerned he is planning something very foolish."

"Like what?"

Aless glanced over at the closed door, and still lowered his voice. "A siege."

"Aless, that's impossible. That would take cunning, guile, planning," he said. "And time. Bundles of time."

"*Sí*. And I've been absent the past three and a half years." Aless stood and went to the window. He could just make out the servants preparing the archery targets. "You've been away at school, me at war. The fact is, we don't know what the Conte has

112

been up to. When I think of the events that unfolded a few years ago—"

"—Surely, you don't believe Padre was responsible for Lady Pricilla's abduction at the Harvest Ball?"

"I don't know what to believe."

"But Francoise DePaul was killed, by Lady Pricilla's own hand, no less." Niccòlo's disbelief raised Aless's hope some. It was true. After DePaul's death everything was thought to have been settled. "Where is all this doubt coming from, Aless? Why are you questioning things from so long ago?"

"The Conte had me meet with him. Quietly."

"Where?" he demanded.

"One location was in the depths of an unused portion of the castle."

"Good heavens, Aless. I pray no one witnessed or overheard any damaging prattle."

Only one person, he thought. He covered in mouth in soft cough. "The point is," he said, determined to stay on course. "If there is any wind of a siege, I don't have to tell you how endangered our position is at Chalmers."

NOW THAT THE CHILDREN were down for their customary afternoon rest, Essie found herself restless with too much time on hand. Cinde was busy with the dressmakers and Cill had adapted to the children's rest schedule. Besides, Cill was much too irritable to spend any time with regardless.

Essie swallowed a sigh and stole down the corridor towards the family library. With all the added guests lurking about, she craved solitude. It had nothing to do with that mind-boggling kiss Alessandro gifted her in the gardens the night before, she admonished silently. But she was unable to stifle the flood of thoughts her mind seemed determined to torture her with. She'd never experienced such sensations that had her near melting into a pool at someone's feet. Were all men's kisses so potent? Or arms so strong and protective?

A surge of anger filled her. The man was a menace toying with her affections after his ruthless declarations to his father. Mayhap she should sample the kiss of others to satisfy her curiosity. Surely, Alessandro de Lecce was not so special.

She slipped into the library where Faustine was sitting before a large fire drinking her tea.

"What irritates you so, *ma chère*?" Never once had Essie heard Sir Arnold's esteemed Maman start a conversation with *bonjour*.

With effort Essie cleared her expression. "My wild imagination." she murmured.

"The children are resting?"

"*Mais oui.*" Essie sighed as a feeling of melancholy swept over her. Confiding her confusion regarding Alessandro to Faustine was a deplorable option. Her feelings were just too jumbled for coherency. Her fingers drifted to her lips where his had touched hers. Slapping his face had never even occurred to her. Speech had deserted her, then her batting eyes sent her scurrying away horrified. She had absolutely no intention of facing him today. She would think of something before the archery match.

"It occurs to me, *ma chère*, that for a young unmarried woman, you spend much of your time with the children. You should be finding a suitable husband. 'Tis obvious you are in need of a family of your own."

Essie scowled, striding to an overstuffed chair near the hearth, and dropped down. In her own best interest she refused to respond to this thread of conversation. Thankfully, she was saved when Sir Arnold stormed into the library. Dark hair, held back in a velvet queue, was escaping its confines. It made him appear somewhat vulnerable. Broad shouldered and tall, like his cousin Prince Charming, Arnald could be a menacing force. His tension was palpable.

"Maman, Lady Esmeralda," he said.

"*Bonjour*, my dear. What troubles you?"

Oh, my. She'd started with *bonjour*, Essie noted. But true to her nature Faustine attacked the matter head on without so much as a breath.

Arnald's gaze moved between Essie and his mother, obviously hesitant to voice his concern.

Essie stood. "If you will excuse me—" she started.

"*Non, non.* Stay." Impatience wreathed from him. He ran a palm over his face and Essie was suddenly concerned for him. His strong features, usually so confident, were lined with worry, jaw tense, lips firmly pressed.

She slowly lowered herself onto the chair.

"I fear my wife is unwell."

"Oh, is that all." Essie breathed in relieved, sinking back.

"Is that all?" Arnald fairly growled. "I am beside myself with worry. She hardly eats, and what she does eat fails to stay with her. I've sent for the surgeon."

Essie looked up, surprised to see both mother and son's tormented expressions. "The surgeon?" The pitch in her tone reached new heights.

"I know naught else to do."

Essie's gaze moved from one then the other. "You do not know?"

"Know what?"Arnald barked and Faustine echoed existing in simultaneous synchronization, no less.

"She is fine, just fatigued," Essie assured the two of them. "It is the way with all women in her condition."

"What condition?" Arnald demanded.

Essie blinked, surprised. "*Enceinte.*"

"*Enceinte,*" Faustine repeated, blankly.

"Expectant? Abundant? Teeming with child..." Their confusion was most aberrant.

Sir Arnald, stunned speechless, just fell back. 'Twas his good fortune the settee sat empty behind.

"You didn't know." It wasn't a question. 'Twas quite clear neither one had had any inkling. Their continued silence became awkward. She sought to reassure them. "'Tis only natural. The symptoms are all there, sickness, irritability, fatigue..." Essie's voice trailed off. Inhaling deeply, she said, "Mayhap you should call off the surgeon—"

Still, they stared at her as if she had two heads. A soft knock at the door startled her.

Theobalde the butler entered, sounding a less than delicate, or possibly reproving, *Ahem.* "My lord, the surgeon has arrived with the leeches. He is ready to bleed your wife."

Both, Faustine and Arnald leaped to their feet. "No!" they yelled.

Chapter 17

A FAIR TO LIGHT COOL breeze filled the west lawn of the castle grounds. The archery tournament was well underway. Lady Pricilla stood poised the next target over, waiting on Aless to complete his shot. The air seemed to agree with her.

Aless drew back on his bow with a slow and leisurely pull. Allowing his thumb to guide the direction along his cheekbone, he pierced the target with a careful aim before spreading his fingers to let the arrow fly. Just inches from the bulls-eye.

"Bravo, *Signore*," Lady Kendra called out. She was part of the small cheering crowd several meters away.

Aless tipped his head in her direction then shifted his attention to his opponent, who was setting her bow. He'd already defeated Joseph.

Heavy footsteps pounded the ground before Niccòlo stormed into his peripheral vision. "I want you to leave her be," he hissed.

So much for the brotherly camaraderie they near experienced earlier that morning. "Will you take a shot?" Aless handed the bow to Niccòlo.

"I just might," Niccòlo growled, clenching one fist. He looked ready to plow Aless in the face. "If you do not see fit to leave her be."

"Lady Esmeralda has no interest in you that I am aware," Aless said blandly.

When Niccòlo blinked in confusion then flashed his dimpled grin, Aless realized he'd made another grand *faux pas*. Granted, this one did not involve as egregious an error as he'd committed two days prior, but it was still an error to a younger brother with a brother's brand of practical humor. No telling what the little *bastardo* would do with the information. Aless refused to acknowledge he could wear that term just as well, and scowled.

Lady Pricilla let go of her arrow. With growing dismay, Aless watched it strike the center of her target.

She'd won.

With grim irritation Aless darted a dark glance to his brother. "Do you suppose Lady Kendra feels the same?" The flush of red creeping up Niccòlo's neck reassured Aless he'd hit his own bulls-eye. "I have no designs on Lady Kendra, my brother. The field is clear for you."

Niccòlo snatched the bow from his outstretched hand and pulled an arrow from the case on Aless's back, all in a move so swift the case did not so much as sway against him. Without any semblance of aim, Niccòlo drew back and fired. The arrow landed so close to the one already stabbed into the target, both shook with the jolt. Niccòlo handed Aless the bow, and without a single added word, swung on his heel and stalked away.

"Touché, my brother." Aless grinned at his retreating form and scanned the area for a certain copper-haired miss, excitement thrumming through him. He'd been disappointed when Lady Esmeralda failed to attend the tournament. And after putting Joseph's efforts to impress her to shame, she had not been there to witness Aless's triumph over his friend.

Lady Kendra, on the other hand, was full of gushing praise.

"I suppose she'll be disappointed to have missed your victory," Joseph said smugly.

Alessandro grunted in response.

"What do you suppose kept her away?" Joseph's bland tone belied his sharp gaze over the lawn just as Aless spotted his quarry some distance away. Lady Esmeralda had both hands fisted at her hips and was smiling at her small charge. Apparently, she and the young prince spent an inordinate amount of time together.

There was no hearing what they conversed from this distance, but just then she shook her head in a firm denial to whatever he'd asked. Laughter split the air, teasing Aless unmercifully. The small prince snagged her hand and they started away from him.

Aless found the sound too irresistible, and somehow his legs were moving in their direction by their own volition.

Joseph alongside him.

"*NON*, YOU MAY NOT try the bow and arrow; you are much too young." Essie grinned at her young charge. She and Edric stood close to the forest and were on their way to the archery tournament where he stubbornly tried to convince her to let him have a turn with a bow. Shading her eyes, she glanced out over the small meadow. Alessandro was priming his bow ready to shoot.

"But you do not have a partner. I would help." Edric was insistent. "Aunt Cill is sick."

"I am not in the tournament, Edric. Aunt Cill is not sick; she is to have a baby. There is a difference. Look," she pointed. "She is about to take her turn. That is beside the point, however." Essie sighed. "Darling, you could not pull the string for the arrow; it would knock you flat." Essie could not contain her laughter at the picture. It would serve him right if she let him try. But then the arrow was sure to stab her in the foot. *Non*, she'd best not chance it.

Edric grabbed her hand. "*S'il vous plaît,* Aunt Sessie?" he begged. "I promise to not hurt myself." He tugged her to a walk.

"Mayhap, 'tis not for you I worry," she smiled.

Edric stopped and looked at her. "Oh," he said. They started walking again, shifting direction, as he seemed to contemplate her words. It appeared she'd gotten through to him, on one issue, leastways.

A cool breeze stirred the murmurings of other voices surrounding them. As she picked out the unmistakable nuances of Spanish or Italian, she often struggled with which one was which, a chilling sensation settled deep within her chest.

"...*niño*..." Boy? Definitely, Spaniards, but they spoke so quickly. Essie cocked her head to one side. Edric tugged at her hand, and mentioned something about picking flowers for his Maman. Oh, why had she not paid closer attention to her Latin text?

"...*que hay que tener; si matas...*" *Must be taken? Kidnapped? Kill?* What was this madness? She darted a sharp gaze over the area as fear teased the hair at her nape. It looked as if Alessandro de Lecce had just parted company with Monsieur Joseph. The Conte's son was making long determined strides straight for her and Edric.

"...*el tiempo es corto...*" *Time is short!* The horror of what she thought she'd heard jarred her into action, fighting to stave off panic.

"*Mon...Dieu,*" she breathed.

"Ow. Aunt Sessie. My hand, *s'il vous plaît.*"

Essie closed her eyes to quell her anxiety. Anyone who had with any inkling of who she was would realize quickly enough at any sudden quips, for now the air was fairly calm. She made a concerted effort to lighten her hold on Edric's tiny hand.

She breathed in deep, praying for composure while at the same time attempted to recognize the voices and determine their direction.

She didn't, and couldn't.

Edric tugged his hand from hers. "I want to hide, Aunt Sessie," he said gleefully, and darted for the trees.

"Edric, don't—" But he was already gone. She took off after him. Her first priority—Edric's safety.

ALESSANDRO CHUCKLED AT HOW he'd manipulated Joseph Pinetti Gray, Viscount Lawrie, future Earl of Yarmouth. Having sent him tarrying after Lady Roche. In essence, he'd killed two birds with one stone. He barely managed to restrain rubbing his hands together.

"Lady Roche is determined you maintain your distance from Lady Esmeralda." Aless had forced a bland tone—one that struck the right balance between "Sorry old man" and "I knew you would not measure up." He'd kept his gaze focused on the woman stationed near the terrace. It worked like a charm.

"We'll see about that," Joseph muttered, before spinning in her direction.

Now all that stood between Lady Esmeralda and he was the expanse of green lawn and the amount of time it took to reach her. Aless narrowed his eyes on Lady Esmeralda and Prince Edric, and lengthened his pace. The silly chit was running into the forest after her small charge.

The sting of brisk wind upped his apprehension, fear prickling his skin. Did he frighten her that badly? The young prince was laughing. His joy pierced the air. Mayhap they played some game.

Well, Aless could play games with the best of them. Yet, he could not stem the notion that danger lay nearby. He broke into a run.

ESSIE'S HEART POUNDED IN her chest. She caught Edric up in her arms and dropped to the ground. She glanced down at him whose curiosity was clearly expressed. Essie put a finger to her lips and tried to smile so as not to alarm him, but she feared it came out more a pained frown. Edric, in all his wise years assured his understanding with a nod and conspiratorial smile.

Now what, she asked herself. They could not stay here all night. Still holding Edric's hand, she tugged him deeper into the forest, and huddled in a clump of bushes. She prayed they would not end up some dangerous animal's snack. The faint murmurings of those men could still be heard, but she was unable to make out their words.

Bien! But now, how was she to spirit Edric away?

Rustling leaves startled her, freezing her to the spot. She stayed Edric with the slight pressure of her hand. She need not have worried, however; he was full into their "game."

"Lady Esmeralda, I know you are here. This is a fool thing you are doing. I would advise you to show yourself." Alessandro's pitch was soft, but the threat was there.

Blast! Startled, she reached forward the mere inches and touched his hand. For a moment, stunned silence reigned. Had those men heard him? She tugged on his hand.

A second later he'd crouched down and was peering at them through the bushes on bended knee. "Prince Edric? Might you need my assistance, *per favore?*"

A soft giggle escaped Edric.

Oh, no. The wind picked up in the trees, there was no help for it. "Shush," she said. His disapproving frown irritated her. At the same time she felt an imminent relief with his presence.

"Might I inquire as to your intentions for this idiocy," Alessandro demanded. Sarcasm colored every inch of his demeanor, from his tone, to the look in his eye.

Rather than answer, Essie clamped a hand over his mouth. The warmth of his breath against her bare palm sent a jolt of desire up her arm through her chest, straight to her flaming cheeks.

The shock in his widened eyes was rather worth it. But she did not believe for one second that he took kindly to her efforts, so with her other hand she put her index finger against her lips.

As the murmurings grew nearer, they became more distinct, as did the language. English now, heavily accented. A frown burrowed in Alessandro's forehead as understanding lit his features. She let out a soft breath.

Through the leaves she could just make out one of the men. "There 'ees no other option. We must kill heem." His disembodied voice was closer now, the accent as heavy as the man.

Essie shuddered, lowered her hand from Alessandro's mouth, which was now a grimace of compressed lips. Her eyes fluttered with anxiety, stirring the trees branches. She squeezed them tightly shut. Did *he* recognize their voices?

With a concentrated effort, she willed her nerves to calm and slowly opened her eyes. She found Alessandro watching her steadily, his gaze unreadable. She could feel the pulse in her neck throb. She pulled Edric close.

In a surprise move, Alessandro covered her fingers with his and pressed.

Chapter 18

IN THE BLINK OF AN EYE, Faustine's dreams were about to come true. Four long years, it had taken for her son and his loving wife to finally give her a *grandchild*. She hardly managed to keep her mind on the conversation at hand. She reveled in the warm blazing fire. Dusk filtered through the windows as the library filled with the family pre-dinner crowd. All but Esmeralda, and the prince and princess were present.

"Where is Essie?" Cill asked.

"I haven't seen her since Edric was attempting to convince her he'd be an ideal partner in the archery contest," Arnald said. "The minute I realized what was afoot, I fled to safety. That child could charm a cobra."

"A cobra, son? An odd analogy," Faustine said.

Pricilla laughed. "She probably worried he would stab her in the foot."

"Surely, she would not allow his participation!" Queen Thomasine exclaimed.

"*Non.* Of course not." Pricilla returned, briskly. "She would worry too much about her *dainty* foot to risk such a deed."

"Tsk, tsk, Pricilla dear. You must let go of your resentment of your sister's smaller extremities." Hilda smiled, but her eyes were calculating.

A deep blush colored Pricilla's cheeks.

The insensitivity of the statement infuriated Faustine. She was tempted to turn the woman into a swine. She gripped the silver baton hidden by her skirts so tightly, she felt a small snap. *Not again*, she thought, swallowing a groan.

Faustine failed to understand Cinderella's oblivion to whatever nefarious thoughts her stepmother harbored, but Faustine saw it as clear as sunrise. It puzzled and frustrated her, this unerring loyalty the princess was determined to maintain towards the sow. Faustine sighed, as she could only vow to do her part in keeping a watchful eye.

"I fear with all the guests arriving, there is no awaiting supper," Thomasine said. "Esmeralda knows I abhor tardiness, most especially for supper. 'Tis our duty as hospitable hosts."

"She knows, Aunt. There is undoubtedly a suitable reason for her lack of punctuality. It usually involves your charming grandson," Arnald assured her.

"He is a handful," Thomasine sighed. "Mayhap, we should we send someone after them."

"Thomasine," Faustine said. "Let the child be. Esmeralda is likely seeing him securely in the nursery as we speak." Despite her words, Faustine felt a twinge of apprehension but she brushed it away. Her own fears were sure to grow now with Pricilla's delicate condition. She prayed she would not prove to be one of those over-the-top ninnies who only focused on what *could* go wrong. After all, she still had her duties as Fairy Godmother. Hilda's actions, leaning on the wrong side of balanced scales, seemed to deepen daily.

Had Cinderella not married Prince, in Hilda's eyes, Esmeralda would be the reigning queen in two weeks time. And to Hilda, blood meant power. Faustine wished that Thomasine could convince Prince to put Lady Roche away, but he would hear of no such thing because his wife refused to contemplate the woman her Papa had married had not done so out of true love.

In Faustine's estimation, Cinderella carried this fairy tale nonsense a bit to the extreme.

Faustine rested her gaze upon Hilda's robust...figure. She simply could not apply the word 'woman' to the red-face, blustering creature.

The clock on the mantel chimed the late hour.

"'Tis time to adjourn to supper," Thomasine said, standing.

Chapter 19

IT SEEMED FOREVER BEFORE the sound of those voices shifted from the vicinity, allowing Essie to breathe.

"They didn't find us, Aunt Sessie," Edric whispered.

"*Oui*, they did not," she said, mildly. She strived not to choke, equally determined to keep Edric from seeing how truly frightened she was.

"I couldn't understand all they said. But I was quiet."

She swallowed, wanting to agree but her voice refused to cooperate.

"You are the King of Hiding, sire," Alessandro offered in her stead.

She could gladly have kissed Alessandro in that moment. The shocking thought embarrassed her, making her fingers tremble. She hugged Edric tightly and pressed her lips to his unruly hair. "*Merci, Signore*," she whispered.

"Why are we whispering, Aunt Sessie?" To her relief Edric seemed content to stay in their game.

"We hide, they must seek," she said.

He nodded eagerly, covering his mouth with his hand.

She pierced Alessandro with narrowed eyes. "Who were they, sir?" She kept her voice mild, cognitive of Edric's natural curiosity.

"I don't know." He frowned, then glanced at the prince. It was clear he wanted to ask who they spoke about, but Alessandro curbed the inclination— admirably so. Instead, he whispered. "We must return. They will be wondering where you and his Highness are."

Essie nodded, but to leave now could place Edric in grave danger. She drummed her fingers on her thigh gathering her thoughts. Nothing brilliant came to mind, however, save for one single idea. She blew out a pursed breath and shot her glance to Edric.

It might work.

THE DARK COVER OF closely knit trees did not begin to dim the sharp intelligence of Lady Esmeralda. The piercing scrutiny she pinned on Aless had him holding his breath. They were in *danger,* yet he reveled in the unexpected isolation of her company. Well, almost, he thought, eyeing the young prince. He'd never get away with kissing her a second time. Not under these circumstances. Although, if Edric told everyone he'd kissed her, mayhap she'd *have* to marry him. The thought was so incongruous his breath hitched. *No,* she'd hate him for certain if she were forced, most especially after his asinine remarks.

Aless watched her closely, wondering if she had any inkling of his mad thoughts. She glanced down at her charge then back up at him. She leaned slowly toward him. Shocked, yet unable to resist, he reciprocated in kind. Her breath touched his ear, sending shivers of sensation down his spine.

"Mayhap, you can go for Prince whilst we wait here." She spoke so matter-of-factly, it took a moment for her meaning to register. So softly spoken, he'd barely heard the words.

And he was outraged. She wanted him to *leave*? The two of them, *unprotected* in the forest? The suggestion was so dimwitted, Aless reared back, fully intending to rail her. But the words stuck in his throat when he grasped Prince Edric's wide-eyed interest. It shifted between Lady Esmeralda and him.

"No one knows where we are," she said warming to her cause. The woman was oblivious to his anger. "We must get word to Prince."

Which only incensed his ire—that she was right. But to leave them in the forest—defenseless? It rubbed against every grain of sound judgment he'd ever harbored. No. He'd find a way back to the castle with his charges in tow. Ha! *The lady was but a girl.* His girl, he decided, wryly.

Aless angled his head and listened for remaining strains of conversation.

Nothing but the rustling leaves.

He rose slowly and risked a look around. Night was descending quickly. Surely, they could come up with a better plan. "Esmeralda—" he whispered urgently.

She addressed him with a lifted brow.

He stifled a groan, managed a steadying breath. "Lady Esmeralda," he started again. "Mayhap we should all make a run for the castle. We are not far from a terrace I discovered only last evening."

"Are we still hiding, Aunt Sessie?" Edric whispered loudly.

"Shush," he and the lady whispered in unison.

"I grow weary of this game, Aunt Sessie," he whimpered.

Alessandro tensed, curious how she would handle Prince Edric's impatience. It was certainly out of his realm of expertise.

She placed both hands on either side of Prince Edric's head. Aless could almost feel the warmth on his own temples. She leaned down, almost nose to nose with him. "Edric," she said softly, eyes serious without so much as a flutter. "Do you trust me?"

The young prince blinked as if surprised by the gravity of her tone. "*Mais oui,* Aunt Sessie." He nodded quickly.

"I fear 'tis imperative we stay hidden a bit longer. I-I..." She took a sustaining inhalation before continuing. "This is of great import, Edric. You must listen to me carefully." Again he nodded, more slowly this time. "We are not playing a game, my darling. I fear there are bad men after us and we must wait for help. Do you understand?"

Rather than answer, he threw his tiny arms round her neck.

Cold infused Aless, and he bit out. "I cannot, nor will I leave the two of you alone."

"*Pardonnez-moi?*" She whispered over Prince Edric's head.

"I *cannot*, and *will not* leave you here alone whilst I go for help," Alessandro told her.

"She will not be alone, *Signore. I* shall protect her," Prince Edric declared. His small chest puffed out in a regal state, a stunning image of his father.

Alessandro could not help but smile at his Highness's dedication to his aunt. How could he not? He felt the same. Aless remained adamant, however. "You are a brave young man, and I've no doubt of your fighting ability, but every man needs another at his side."

The prince's chest rose proudly, at having been called a man, or that he could fight. Aless knew not which.

"But, either we all leave together, or we all wait together."

"*Signore, pardonnez-moi,* you must. Surely you see we cannot stay amidst the elements all night?"

"'Tis my final say on the matter," Aless said calmly.

"I'm frightened, Aunt Sessie." Edric's meek voice quickly reminded Alessandro the child was only four.

"Oh, Edric." Esmeralda pulled his head to her shoulder, cradling it in a protective palm.

"What have you to be frightened of, sire? I am a warrior and you are a prince. Together, we are here to serve and protect our fair maiden. *No?*"

The little prince twisted his head to peer at him, never lifting his head from Esmeralda's shoulder. "You mean she is like Lady Marian and you, Sir Robin Hood, and me Little John? Though *John* was not so little." His eyes were as big as saucers. "Nor, am I," he saw fit to add.

Alessandro may have overplayed it a bit, but shrugged. What did it hurt if the child considered him a hero of such proportions? And he had no trouble visualizing Lady Esmeralda as Maid Marian. The damsel in distress, sitting back on her heels in her dark green dress, copper tendrils brushing her forehead, and child in her lap. 'Twas a charming picture.

Esmeralda hid her face in the young prince's wild, windblown locks, her shoulders trembling.

"*Per favore* do not worry so, milady. I vow I speak the truth." Alarm seared Aless at the intensity of her anxiety. Yet he glanced around, surprised the wind remained relatively calm.

The prince pushed away from her shoulders and Aless's gaze followed Edric's, drawn in by the fiery brilliant depths of her eyes. They seem to light up the night sky, stealing his breath. A delicate snort sounded. Most definitely a snort.

Aless pierced her with narrowed eyes. Laughing. She was *laughing*.

"You are laughing? Aunt Sessie?" Edric said, echoing Aless's thoughts.

"The Sheriff of Nottinghamshire, more like," she hiccupped, obviously trying to cover her hysterics, drawing a giggle from the prince. In that moment, Alessandro vowed he would ne'er call her Lady Esmeralda again, save for polite company. She was Esmeralda to him, now.

Certainly not once they married. And when had he decided that?

Chapter 20

PRICILLA STOOD IN THE middle of her bed chamber and turned slowly. She was trying to decide if her dinner of roast potatoes and grilled lamb agreed with her unusually stout appetite, or if she should dive for the chamber pot beneath the bed. She breathed short, shallow breaths.

"No one has heard nary a word from either of them. Something is wrong. I know it," she insisted. Irritability pricked under her skin like a thorn she could not get out of her shoe. She paused before the looking glass and scowled at her unruly blond curls and pale cheeks. "'Tis by the grace of God, Cinde and Prince were scheduled to meet with the prince of Spain and his new bride."

"Your sister is playing hide and seek with him. Or helping him with his bath," Arnald assured her. "You know how she adores the children."

"Unlike me, you mean?" What was this need she had to quarrel, she wondered furiously.

The maids had laid a roaring fire to ward off the evening chill. But Pricilla found it stifling, *suffocating*. She should pull out the chamber pot. Instead, she strode to the window and fought through the heavy fabrics. Latch, she needed the latch. If she did not soon breathe fresh air...

"*Non.* That is not what I meant, *ma chère*," he said from behind. "You are choosing to read more into my words than I say. 'Tis a flaw you cannot help when you are under duress."

She spun to give him the full brunt of her ire, but found herself quickly entangled with no way out. The curtains needed airing. Dust motes filled her nostrils, gagging her. "Flaw!" she sputtered.

Strong sure moves quickly disassembled her captivity in efficient effort.

Her husband flipped the latch on the window and shoved it open. "Duress," he corrected with a quick kiss to her brow.

She gave him a reluctant smile. "Duress, then." Then she narrowed her eyes on him. "Don't think your compellation powers are working on me, my lord."

"I would never." He drew a cross over his heart.

Forgetting the sudden need for air, Pricilla put a hand to her stomach. "Will you still love me when I am fat?"

"That is a trick question, and well you know it." Arnald lifted her chin and looked her in the eye. "Are you that disappointed in carrying my child?" His gentle tone nearly undid her, filling her eyes with tears.

She touched her palm to his jaw, touched by the naked fear she read in his gaze. "In truth, I am terrified," she whispered. "Cinde almost died if, you recall."

"*Oui,* I recall. But she did not. Do not forget my Maman is quite the herbalist."

"Humph," she muttered under her breath.

He pulled her close. "Well," he consoled, "Mayhap it will give you comfort to know that 'tis *I* who will look after you, not she."

"*Oui.*" Pricilla smiled and laid her head against his shoulder. "That gives me great comfort. I think I'd feel better if I checked on Edric..."

Chapter 21

"THE SHERIFF, HUH?" ALESSANDRO grunted. "'Tis obvious I have not yet convinced you of my sincere regrets."

Essie gulped deep breaths to keep her laughter from turning to hysterics, then to tears. The loss of control teetered on the edge of her sanity.

"I-I'm sorry, but *Robin Hood*?" she choked out, eyeing his lace cuffs. She could just make out the polished buttons on his waistcoat. Hardly a man prone to steal from the rich to give to the poor. At least his boots were not reflecting the shine of the moon.

Alessandro lifted a brow. She took in the strong line of his jaw, his now tousled windswept hair, and swallowed. He could have been a warrior, she realized. He reeked of untold mystery, sitting on his knees in the depths of the forest, vowing his protection.

Bah! He was also a man who prejudged an intelligent woman. Just because she might get a bit nervous on occasion—surely she was not the *only* girl with a windstorm affliction that could set a man off his feet.

A cool shift of air touched her arms making Edric shiver. It jolted her back to their present dilemma. Essie hugged Edric tighter, wishing...wishing...she blew out a pursed breath. One of defeat. What was the use of wishing? She was not the one with a fairy godmother, *non*?

Let Alessandro defend their lives just as he'd proffered. 'Twas their only hope at the moment encased with his stubborn Italian pride.

"My lord, forgive me, *s'il vous plaît*." She fairly choked, getting the words past the disgust in her throat. "I fear the situation is playing havoc with my senses. I bow to your greater wisdom in this matter." The gods were smiling on her, leastways, as lightning did not bolt from the sky to strike her dead. More likely due to the dense cover of the forest.

Alessandro watched her steadily.

Stretched silence had her tempting to squirm. But intuition told her looking away would be a mistake. She offered him a bland expression instead. Willed her eyes to focus, remain steady. She found if she concentrated, she was quite able to control the incessant fluttering. She blinked as a sudden thought struck. Perhaps that was the message the elder Chevalier Pinetti had tried to convey. Of course, it made perfect sense!

Despite their current predicament, a lightness filled Essie's heart she hadn't felt since she, Cinde, and Cill had turned friends rather than foes. She blinked again finding Alessandro still studying her, his gaze impenetrable.

After an interminable moment, he nodded once; apparently, accepting her acquiescence, and moved clear of their hiding place. He crouched close to the ground, a distinct growl sounding from him. "The sheriff, indeed."

She grinned at his back.

Chapter 22

THE DOOR BOUNDED BACK against the wall. "What is it, *ma chère?* You are breathless." Arnald caught Pricilla by the arms. Fear emanated from her in waves. Night had fallen early after a long and trying day. Prince and Princess Cinderella had not yet returned from their visit with the Spanish nobleman. But Arnald knew Prince felt strong undercurrents; and as Spain was their closest ally, he had to agree with the decision to humor them.

Responsibilities and the pressure of the king's death weighed heavy on his cousin's shoulders. Arnald stemmed the misgivings suddenly swarming him. Surely, it was just the strangers milling the castle that had him jittery. He'd looked forward to spending a quiet evening with his adorable wife. He wanted to rub her back and revel in the knowledge that she carried his child. In another week, once preparations for the coronation ceremony became insurmountable, free time would cease to exist.

The heavy drapes of their private living quarters were drawn for the evening. "He is not there!" Her startled cry ripped through the chamber.

"Who, my darling?" Alarm tingled up his spine. Pricilla was not prone to hysterics.

"Edric," she screamed. "No one has seen Edric."

"He is surely with Esmeralda," he soothed.

"I've just returned from the nursery. He is not there and she has not been seen since late this afternoon. We must do something." She pounded her fists against his chest as uncontrollable sobs tore from her. They echoed against the chamber walls. "We must do something. Do you realize what this will do to Cinde?" She fell to her knees. "We have to do something...find him..."

"Darling—"

"*Non*," she growled, shoving the tears from her face. "I felt something was amiss. I should have waylaid my qualms hours ago." She looked up at him, determination set in her chin. "*You* shall call out the dogs."

Something broke inside Arnald's chest. Something akin to his heart. "*Certainement.*" He lifted her from the floor, pressed a hard kiss to her forehead and strode from the room determined to set her mind at ease, no matter the cost. She was right. His nephew was the heir to the throne, and his cousin's child. He was a fool to not have listened before now.

Chapter 23

THE CHILL IN THE air grew denser with each moment passing. Somehow Alessandro had to get the young prince and his enigmatic aunt to the castle. He stayed low to the ground, alert for anything that implied a threat.

The accented voices Esmeralda had stumbled upon were undeniably Italian intermingled with Spanish, he grimaced. 'Twasn't Cuneo, *his* home, however. He would swear to it. He would have recognized its distinct dialect. It seemed more in line with the central portion of his beloved country. Still, the question begged an answer, who did they mean to kill, and why—barking dogs split the silent air with a sudden violence.

Perspiration dampened his back, even in the cool night air. Fear clogged his senses. *The war is over.* He repeated the silent mantra. But somehow the stampede of the ground rattled the teeth in his head, the clanking of metal swords as an army swarmed ahead. Flickering flames flared in balls of blinding yellows, reds and orange. He was dizzy with visions of war.

Throat dry, Aless reached for his blade shocked to find himself unarmed. Panic swelled through him. He could not have lost his sword, he would have remembered. He shook his head, but the vibrating ground pounded over the beating in his chest...

"Signore de Lecce?"

Alessandro reached furiously toward that call. He tugged at the cloth around his neck. It choked him. He tried to respond. *Dio*, why would his voice not cooperate?

"Sir? Alessandro?"

They were on him now...someone had his sleeve. He shoved it away in a weak effort to escape. His face flamed in the cool night air, yet the heat of fire moved ever closer. Panic threatened to swallow him. *Where was his sword? He never fought without his sword.*

"Aunt Sessie?" Edric cried, though it was quiet.

"Do not worry, *ma chère*. We shall be fine," she whispered. The earth quaked beneath her knees, prompting Essie into action. She refused to die a sitting duck. "Stay close, but behind."

Edric nodded his understanding before she set him to her side. On all fours, she crept forward from the false safety of their sheltered hiding place, mimicking Alessandro's movements, keeping low as well as she was able in a full set of skirts. She feared her green velvet was all but done for.

Edric obeyed, staying behind, occasionally catching her skirts between his small hand or knee and the ground. So she kept her movements small.

Her gaze was caught by the brilliance of light ahead. Not the subtle glow of a thousand candles; but the raging flames of torches. Hundreds of them.

Mon...Dieu. Prince had sent out the hounds! And the regiments! She almost wept with joy. They were safe. Help was on the way. Thank heavens. She crawled faster.

But as relief sailed over her, she caught the silhouette of Alessandro's shadowed figure still crouched, panic searing his features as he searched the ground about him. She looked from him to the horde of soldiers, then back again. Did he see something she did not?

Something was wrong. Essie moved to his side. "Signore de Lecce?" she called softly.

He clawed at the cravat round his neck. His gaze met hers but 'twas if he didn't recognize her. It filled her with a coldness the night air couldn't match.

"Alessandro?" She grabbed his arm, fear pumping the blood through her veins.

He pushed her hand away as if she were a pesky fly. The shock, anxiety, and apprehension that reverberated over her sent her eyes fluttering into a surge of wind so powerful, it knocked him back—flat on his backside.

"Oh," Essie gasped. Horrific dismay rendered her immobile. "*Je suis désolée.*"

Alessandro sat up slowly, shaking his head. He took in the scene around them as if he were just seeing the situation.

"Are you quite all right, my lord?"

"*Si, si.*"

But he did not appear all right to her. She might be unable to discern the paleness in his face with the fiery torches, but his compressed lips showed a strain even the black of night could not veil. Nor the clenched fists or drawn shoulders. As much as she desired, she dare not touch him, the rejection would be beyond humiliating.

Barking dogs grew more raucous. It appeared just the ruse to jar Alessandro to his feet. He held out his hand. She hesitated. But his eyes cleared and he seemed himself once more.

"Come, milady, sire. It appears we're about to be discovered."

Before Essie could decide whether or not she could suffer any more embarrassment, Edric bounced to his feet like an excited rabbit. He darted around Alessandro, but Alessandro proved too quick, even for the likes of Edric. His arm shot out and he caught him by the waist.

Essie almost smiled.

"Not to worry, sire. The dogs have us in their line now. 'Tis only a matter of moments," Alessandro told him, softly. His eyes glittered in the darkness on Essie, and she found herself unable to look away.

"But—"

"Edric," Essie said sharply.

"*Merci, Signore*," he said meekly.

"LOOK, AUNT SESSIE, 'TIS Uncle Arnald," Edric called out.

The first thing Essie noticed when she emerged from the woods was relief on Sir Arnald's face, mingled with fear, followed by absolute fury. Oh, not directed at her. But based on the glint in his eye, Alessandro was the casualty to bear the brunt of power Arnald was certain to mete out.

Arnald made straight for Edric, snatching him from Alessandro's arms with a violence that frightened Essie. "Arrest this man!" he barked.

Stunned to a frozen stupor, Essie gaped in horror as the shifting, grating metal of drawn swords saturated the night; a dawning moment to realize Alessandro relinquished his freedom, no word of argument forthcoming.

Why did he not fight? Why did he not speak?

"Take him from my sight," Arnald commanded. Before Essie could grasp a breath, He had her in a firm grasp and was heralding her up the path.

"What are you do—" she started.

"Quiet, milady," he growled. His wrath was now fully directed on her.

"But—"

He pulled her up by the arm. "Enough!"

Truly terrified, she surely would have taken flight had he not had such an unyielding grip. The branches in the trees swayed in protest to the sudden torrent that swept the air. This was completely out of character. Why was he so angry with her and Alessandro? They'd saved Edric, kept him safe. She needed to tell him what she'd overheard.

"Uncle, some bad men—"

"*Mais oui*, son, I know. You are safe now." Amazement seared Essie at the gentleness he offered Edric, while pulling her along without so much as a hitch in his breath or stride. All the while he carried Edric's solid form. She had to run to stay abreast. No doubt had she tripped Arnald would have dragged her along the ground like a broken rag doll.

"Sir—"

"I said enough, Lady Esmeralda."

They slipped through the terrace doors that led to her and her sisters' secret sitting chamber. Arnald stopped and turned to the closest brute at hand. He practically tossed her into the surf's massive grip where she had not a hope of escape. The indignity of it stung.

"See her to her chamber. No one is to enter."

"*Oui*, my lord." The deep resonance spelled captive to Essie, not comfort.

Arnald turned a cold glare on her, confirming the thought. "You shall be dealt with in good time." To her utter degradation, Arnald spun away without even the courtesy of an acknowledgement.

She sputtered a protest, but he was already rounding the corner from sight.

"Night, Aunt Sessie," Edric called out over his shoulder, waving no less.

"*Mademoiselle*? This way, *s'il vous plaît*," The brute murmured. She snatched her arm from him and stomped down the corridor to her chambers.

No one to enter? Hah! She gave a grim smile. There was no command on an exit, was there?

WELL, THAT WENT REMARKABLY different than he'd envisioned. Alessandro scrubbed a palm over his face, wondering how he'd managed such a quick status tumble from hero in the eyes of young Edric. Ah, not to forget the accusation of being Robin Hood's nemesis to Esmeralda. There wasn't much chance of changing her opinion, jailed in the depths of dung. The surprise, then outrage he'd witnessed in her eyes when Sir Arnald ordered his arrest was comforting, if not much help. He blew out a steady breath. Now, he'd landed as prisoner in Chalmers for God-knew-what.

Alessandro stood and circled slowly, determined to strategize his next move. The damp, musty smell was rank enough. Intermingled with urine in his current accommodations indicated the prince's cousin was definitely not sympathetic to his cause. He rattled the barred door. Considerably difficult under the current conditions—giving nary an inch. Had he expected any different?

With one fist on his hip, Aless circled and faced the back of his tiny blocked space, and pushed fingers through his hair, frustrated. No window. 'Twas obvious Sir Arnald deemed him the lowest of the low. A womanizing, child abductor—one could not go much lower than that. He'd only thought to offer the knight a moment of cooling off when he'd read the rage in his gaze.

An unexpected scrape of metal echoed against the stone surfaces. A key creaked in the lock, the effort laborious. *Now what?*

The cell door moved inward and Aless awaited his visitor unannounced visit with undue patience.

Chapter 24

NOW THAT EDRIC WAS secured in his own bed, Pricilla more reassured, she looked at her husband, shocked. "You did *what*?"

Arnald paced, and said, "He is below stairs."

"In the *dungeon*?" Pricilla could not believe what her ears were surely telling her.

"*Certainement.*"

"And Essie?" she demanded.

"In her chambers." Her husband spoke mildly, but she knew it to be a ruse.

"Did you happen to ask what happened?"

"My concern was in retrieving Edric. Reassuring *you* of his safety." He was defensive, a sure sign he knew he'd wronged. "I lost my temper."

"Rare, indeed," she acknowledged. Then grimaced. "I must speak with her right away. You may as well accompany me. You shall be eating a big black crow."

"Might I remind you they had Edric, heir to the throne, the future of this kingdom? You were terrified." He stopped, then said, "I suppose I owe *her* an apology."

Pricilla reached up and brushed her husband's lips with her own. "*Mais oui*, my love. But all is not lost yet. Although, Cinde would have your head." Pricilla aimed for the door. "Essie would *never* steal Edric, my dear." Nor would Alessandro de Lecce, she would stake her life on it. The thought was so ludicrous a burst of laughter escaped.

"You are determined to right this tonight?"

"Of course, tonight. This certainly cannot possibly wait until morning. 'Twould be disastrous."

"*Ma chère,* surely—"

"*Non!*" The horrific mistreatment of Essie was abominable. He didn't understand how delicate Cinde felt the relationship was with her sisters. Pricilla strode through the corridor relentless in her mission. "We've no time to lose." She rounded the corner where a burly man stood. "*You posted a guard?*" She almost shrieked but caught herself in time to murmur her outraged disbelief. "*Mon...Dieu!* 'Tis incredible," she muttered under her breath. She gave the guard a brilliant smile. Difficult with her churning insides.

She could feel Arnald dogging her heels. Likely, she, Cinde and Essie would find humor in the situation on the morrow. Leastways, she prayed that would be the case.

In the meantime, however...

Pricilla pulled up before the guard, and tapped her foot. A resigned sigh from Arnald preceded his less than sharp command to the wary-eyed ward. "Stand aside, sentinel. We wish to enter."

It took every ounce of practiced regality to resist shoving the armored man aside. Not that she could have budged him an inch. He was massive, but the urge toward something violent was fierce.

"Has anyone entered, sir?"

"*Non,* my lord, just as you instructed. But I confess to hearing strange noises."

"Strange noises?" He shook his head. "*Merci,* my good man. You are dismissed."

With a sharp bow the guard quickly dispersed.

Pricilla shoved fallen hair from her brow. She turned the knob and stepped into her sister's chamber. The sight that met her eyes could not be borne, and she groaned. "I fear we too late, my darling."

Clothes were strewn haphazardly about. An open window fluttered the curtains in the cool night breeze, not of Essie's doing.

She was nowhere in sight.

"WELL, WELL, WELL," ARNALD said. "Where do you suppose the little spitfire is?"

"Don't call her a spitfire." Pricilla snapped. "Essie is obviously upset."

"Darling, mayhap you should rest," he soothed.

Pricilla glared at him before letting out a frustrated sigh. "You don't understand, for too many years Essie and I were not the most congenial of sisters. I could not bear it if things were to return to that unspeakable time. Cinde certainly could not."

Arnald wrapped his arms about her, pulling her into his chest. "I suppose I could have overreacted. Your concern when no one had seen Edric, coinciding with de Lecce's appearance from the woods with him in his arms—well, I fear I wanted to kill him."

She couldn't help it, she smiled against his chest. "*Oui,* I suppose you could have at that," she said softly.

Heaving a deep breath he set her from him, lifted her chin to meet his gaze. "'Tis my life's duty to see you suffer naught, *ma chère.*"

She closed her eyes as he touched her lips in the brush of a feathery kiss. "But I suppose there must be some explanation for his presence."

Pricilla opened her eyes and grinned. "Mayhap you should see to the matter promptly, *oui?* But hear him out before you wrap your fingers about his throat, *s'il vous plaît.*"

"'Twill be difficult, I assure you. Return to our quarters and I shall meet you there. And not a word to a soul. Surely, the night will still manage some salvageability." His wicked grin sent a shiver of delight over her, infusing warmth to her cheeks. She followed him to the hall. Shaking her head at the wonder of her blessings, she turned for the opposite direction.

ALESSANDRO BLINKED. THEN BLINKED again, his eyes surely deceiving him, feet rooted to stone floors. The cold in the cell seeped into his bones.

"I fear we must make haste, *Signore*." He heard the words, the breathy voice, inhaled the familiar fragrance. Lavender, if he were not mistaken. None of it reconciled with the sight standing before him. A dark hat hid any shred of copper curl, and a great coat, wool and practical, swarmed the small body beneath. His gaze moved down where he fathomed he could make out black boots.

"Make haste?" he repeated.

"We must go," she said, not without impatience. "I have a prince to protect. Either you are with me or you are not."

"With you?" He shook his head, apparently unable to comprehend the words even though they rang out crisp and distinct. Finally, common sense snapped into place. "Are you mad?"

"I suppose that is a possibility, sir. Prince Charming shall thank me—us, later. Come, you are wasting time."

Oh, Dio. He supposed she had a point. If Aless did not see fit to leave her in the forest alone with a small child, he felt more so now, witnessing the determination that glittered in the sharp emerald gaze.

Obviously, when they married, they would be leaving Chalmers long behind—most likely with an army of guards on their heels.

"I see I have no option in the matter," he growled, stepping through the cell door. This escapade would seal his fate one way or another— either married to the lovely Esmeralda, or his lifeless body hanging at the end of a rope.

It didn't take long to reach the deserted portion of the castle, but they didn't stay there long as the hall turned more livable. Aless stayed close on her heels. This whole idea of hers was fraught with danger. But apparently, there was no stopping his adventurous soon-to-be-wife when that stubborn chin of hers decided on a course of action, he was learning. He had no choice but to find some way to save her pretty little neck.

Finally, after so many twists and turns he thought he would expire from dizziness, he felt compelled to comment. "You do have a plan in mind?" he whispered.

"Of course, I do," she snapped.

He waited to see if more information was forthcoming. Nothing.

"Esmeralda," he started.

When she stopped so abruptly, forcing him to steady her from tumbling forward, he thought she might be startled by his informal address. Then he heard it—the unmistakable urgency of low tones firing off rapid Spanish.

She turned to him with pleading eyes, then stood on the tips of her toes and whispered in his ear. "They are speaking too quickly. I can't understand what they are saying."

With a finger to her lips, he leaned into her, lavender assaulting his senses, a welcome change from his recent accommodations. "They are searching for the nursery. They believe they are in the right wing," he whispered.

She stiffened. Her reaction confirmed her assumption.

Aless counted three different voices. "How close are we?" he asked.

Panic showed in her eyes and at once they picked up in their flutter. He pulled her head into his shoulder to stem the brisk upsweep that would give way their location.

"Four doors," she breathed against his shirt.

He felt every heated breath. "We need a distraction." An incredible thought slammed through him. And with only seconds to implement such an outrageous idea, he lifted her chin and focused intently on her. It was not so difficult. The hardship, he knew, would be in tearing his gaze away.

She shifted, uncomfortable under his scrutiny.

Aless tightened his grip. He and Joseph's harmless pranks from school might serve him well. Those little games where each of their friends sat in a circle and tried their best to out-maneuver one another with mind control? Sometimes with interesting results.

Esmeralda struggled to pull away but he held her steady, dropped his gaze to her lips. Plump, red, luscious, those lips—and so tempting. He hovered just above not daring to touch, lest he lose sight of his goal. In the end, he was unable to resist a small taste, and let the tip of his tongue graze her. He skimmed the softness of her cheek with his knuckles.

Quite suddenly, his plan took flight.

Windows at the far end of the corridor burst open with a blast of wind from her nervous phenomenon. The gust startled the sputtering trio, and the strength of that gale knocked them clear of their path.

"*Dio!*" Alessandro breathed in surprise. "'Tis a powerful weapon you wield, *Tesoruccio.*" He almost laughed at the shock-turned-suspicion in her narrowed eyes.

For a moment she appeared speechless. But her natural impertinence quickly asserted itself. "What did you call me?"

He tapped her nose with the tip of his finger and handed her a wicked grin. "Cute little treasure. Now, lead the way," he nudged her.

She blinked, appearing uncertain. But in an unexpected action that had him inhaling sharply, she grinned briefly just before she stood on the tips of her toes, touched her lips lightly to his, then spun and darted down the corridor.

Chapter 25

WIPING THE WORRY FROM Pricilla's brow was strong motivation, Arnald smiled. He rounded the corner and picked up his step, set to hand Alessandro de Lecce his reprieve. Taking all but ten minutes he found himself standing before an open, *empty* cell door, keys dangling from the lock.

That certainly answered the question of Lady Esmeralda's disappearance, Arnald grimaced. He felt a touch of wry, at her rebellion, however; allowing to himself some situations had a tendency to right themselves. Visconte Alessandro de Lecce would find himself attached to the rebellious maiden rather soon once Prince got wind of this little escapade.

Arnald sprung up the stairs. Now he had to tell his wife what her sister had accomplished. No telling where Esmeralda led the unsuspecting Alessandro. And he had no doubt who had led whom. After all, he was married to one of the three wily creatures. Not that anyone could convince him to trade his wife for another. A surge of pity at what the poor man was up against swept through him, drawing a bark of laughter.

A moment of dark crowded his churning thoughts. What if they'd eloped? He pushed away that incongruent thought. Lady Esmeralda would never desert the princess, not for something as so important as Prince's coronation to king.

Mayhap de Lecce enticed her against her will. *Non, non.* That didn't sit well either. Lady Esmeralda was much too stubborn to be convinced against her will. Then what? She would be appalled to realize how well they all knew her deepest feelings regarding the Conte's elder son.

Arnald strode down the corridor, thoughts swirling. Of course, he was obligated to apprise Prince of the situation. The undercurrents were too prevalent. He reached the door of his chambers with no explanations for his wife.

He pushed through the archway and saw her pacing to and fro. "Darling, you shall need to dress, we've a situation," Arnald said.

She stopped. "What situation?" she demanded.

"Alessandro is missing."

"Don't be ridiculous. He was behind bars, was he not? It was locked, I assume."

Arnald watched, fascinated, the various expressions fleet across her face—Surprise, irritation, resolve.

"And Essie, is gone as well," she stated, slowly. "She always did clamor for all the attention," Pricilla said, disgusted. "Where do you suppose *she* is?" Pricilla fisted her hands at her hips. It occurred to Arnald these three sisters could take out an army with demeanor alone. A slow grin touched her lips. "She shall have to marry him."

"Most likely so, I suspect."

"In any event, the drama should play out in an entertaining fashion." Her grin was quickly replaced by a frown. "Unless Maman discovers it first," she said under her breath. She glanced up quickly. "Have you given any thought to their whereabouts?"

"Some."

She narrowed her eyes on him.

"The thought occurred to me that they may have eloped."

A grim frown furrowed her features. "That is unlikely."

Arnald waited. When she offered nothing further on that cryptic statement, he said. "I fear I shall have to inform my cousin."

She began her pace once more. "Have Prince and Cinde returned from their visit with the Spanish heir and his bride? When are they due back?"

Arnald shook his head, trying to sort out the rapid interrogation. "No one knows how long these things take. They've already been gone the entire day."

She glanced up quickly. "What about Cinde? My first inclination is save her this worry for now. She is prone to hysterics. And what of Edric?"

"*That,* my love, is a *very* good question."

Chapter 26

"MAKE HASTE, ESSIE."

"Don't you think it somewhat juvenile to refer to me by a pet name?" she demanded softly.

"Shush, you'll wake the whelp," Alessandro whispered. "Besides, I didn't call you *Sessie*. I called you Essie. Isn't that how your closest near-and-dears refer to you?" He hid a grin at her compressed lips, surely caused by his reference to Edric as a whelp. And they did need to make haste. It was probably the only reason she restrained from calling him out. He had no doubt she was a crack shot.

Aless grabbed her hand and tugged her through Edric's parted door keeping her to the safety of his back. "I fear your plan was not well thought out, Essie. I thought you said this was Prince Edric's room."

"What are you talking about?" she hissed. "It is."

He pointed to the empty bed. "If you did not miscount the doors, I fear we have a slight problem. He's not here."

"Of course, he...he's here. He...he's just hide...hiding." She dropped to her knees and peered beneath the bed. Alessandro opened the wardrobe. More shoes than any child of four could possibly use in one lifetime lined the shelves in perfect order.

Esmeralda heaved deep sudden gulps. He swung round and kneeled before her. She was rooted to the floor, slight body swaying.

"Shallow breaths, my lady," he cautioned. She was clearly on the verge of an all out swoon. Aless clamped a hand on the back of her head, knocking her odd looking cap askew. "That's it, Darling," he whispered. "Take it slow."

Her small frame shivered with uncontrollable racks. "Where could he have gone? How shall we find him?" Gasps of panic had her voice rising, and with it, a real threat of passing out. "We have...to...find...him. If we can make it to Cill or Cinde's chambers we...we could tell them what we overheard..." she hiccupped.

Alessandro pulled her face into his shoulder, effectively blocking her air flow. It quieted her but the heat of her breath seeped through the thin lawn of his shirt, startling him. "An excellent notion," he said. He should have thought of it sooner. It was the perfect solution.

"What?" she muffled against his shirt. Satisfied she'd once more garnered control, he leaned her from him. "He is just a small child." He tilted her chin with an index finger and found her eyes glistening with tears. They shimmered like rare jewels in the in the blunted moonlight through the sheer linings covering the windows.

"I'll find him, my lady."

She steeled her spine, straightened her shoulders before whispering. "You?" She narrowed her eyes on him, but he heard a suspicious sniff. "You know nothing of his likes, dislikes, his fears, his habits. He might be terrified—" Panic rose in her voice again.

"Enough, we must keep calm, lest we wake the nursemaid." he growled. Obviously, there was no convincing her he could handle the search on his own. He had a feeling he there would not be much he'd be able to deny her, now or in the future. He took a calming breath. "Then we must devise a plan, Essie."

That drew a watery smile on her part—and if he were honest, a bit of relief on his.

"Come, time is of the essence."

Chapter 27

THE MORNING SUN BURST through the castle with the fortitude of a stubborn goat—a bleating goat. Pricilla gave a languid stretch her arm grazing the empty place where a sleeping body should have lain.

She sat up so quickly her head spun. She breathed short shallow breaths to right herself. Where was Arnald? He'd been gone all night? Before she could fathom a reason for his absence, a furious pounding to the adjoining door to her husband's chamber sounded.

"Enter."

Arnald's grim face appeared around the door. The set of his shoulders sent a trickle of dread over her skin.

"What is it?" she demanded.

Her husband looked as if he'd not rested at all, which of course, he hadn't. His eyes were bloodshot and hair askew. 'Twas not in keeping with his cousin's princely image.

"I've seen no sign of Esmeralda or Alessandro de Lecce, darling. Furthermore, Edric has disappeared from his bed. There are broken windows in the children's wing."

"But—" Pricilla stopped mid sentence and shook her head. "Do you suppose she eloped?" Then gasped. "I don't suppose you thought to check to see if Chevalier Pinetti is missing too? He was most attentive towards her when he pulled his magician's trickery."

"This is disturbing," he said. "I don't know what to think. Edric's disappearance raises the stakes considerably."

"Essie would never harm Edric. That thought is ludicrous. Furthermore, I refuse to believe she would disappear before the coronation ceremony," she said curtly." Leastways, not intentionally."

"While I concur completely, there is still the matter of the missing heir." Arnald's grim tone spelled disaster as he dropped beside her on the bed.

Pricilla looked over at him. "What do you propose? And what of the nursemaid? Surely she noticed her little charge missing."

"First and foremost, we cannot let this go any further than you and I. Leastways, until I speak with my cousin."

She nodded slowly, understanding filling her. "You are thinking of the smuggled arms we stumbled across several years past, are you not?"

"*Oui*," he said softly.

Pricilla clutched his hand. "But, darling, that was five years ago. DePaul is dead." She shuddered. "I-I killed him, m-myself." He returned the squeeze on her hand. The gesture was meant to be reassuring.

Unfortunately, his words were anything but. "Plenty of time for our nemesis to have reinforced their plans, whatever they are. Plenty of time for Chalmers to have relaxed their guard." Arnald stood and pulled her to her feet, dropping a kiss on her nose. "Get dressed. We've a child to locate, and not much time. My cousin is liable to behead us. Even more frightening? Your sister, skinning each and everyone us all alive."

Chapter 28

ESSIE GROANED, AND MOVED her head side to side. Why was she so sore? And why was her bed so warm, yet uncomfortable?

"How's your neck?"

She started at the husky resonance of Alessandro's voice piercing the darkness. His whispered words stirred the hair on her neck

"That good? I'm not surprised by that angle in which you slumbered. We must make haste, Essie."

Slowly events from the early morn pierced her fog-filled brain. The bed was uncomfortable because she was hiding in an old wardrobe due to the lingering presence of a couple of late-night servants. She absolutely refused to speculate on what had kept those two lingering in the deserted chamber. The last thing she recalled was a lot of silly giggling and Alessandro pulling her back against his chest. It was warm and snug—inappropriately so.

Their precarious position shocked her senses momentarily before common sense pervaded, and she scurried away from him. "Sir!" Unfortunately, her voice came out strangled and incoherent. She tried again. She ran fingers through her disheveled curls. "M-must you call m-me by that juvenile name?" Dust kicked up from the floor, had her eyes squeezing shut. Mortification pounded her veins.

Morning sun streamed through a crack beneath the door. As her eyes adjusted to the low light she could see the devilish grin he flashed her was positively wicked.

They'd combed several of Edric's favorite hiding places, to no avail. She cringed. *She'd just spent the night with Alessandro de Lecce.* She peeked at him through the hair covering her face.

Still grinning, Alessandro gave a leisurely stretch. "And how would you have me refer to you? A young, *virtuous* woman with whom I have just spent the night?"

She glared at him, before spotting her knitted cap just within reach. She snatched it up and shoved her hair under it. The small task allowed her to avoid his scrutiny.

"'Tis first light and I fear we need a plan of action."

"First light," she repeated. *Mon...Dieu.* They would make her marry the cur. She stared into the dark eyes boring into hers. Dark growth stubbled his jaw, indicating just how intimate the situation had turned. The sight froze Essie. Her gaze moved to his firm lips that had dared to touch hers. The tip of her tongue swiped at her own dry lips and she swallowed.

"Essie?" Alessandro whispered. His eyes were trained on her mouth. "'Tis what your sisters call you. It suits you. And me referring to you as such, I think. Essie slides easily from my tongue."

He lifted his eyes to meet hers. "*Oui*," she said.

"A plan then, Essie?"

"*Oui,* a plan," she repeated.

"Where else might our little prince hide?" he prodded.

Essie shook her head to gather her thoughts, breaking the hold Alessandro de Lecce seemed to have on her. "Edric? *Oui*, Edric. He...he likes to hide."

"*Si*, but where?" he said. "You do not believe he would leave the castle?"

"*Non*. He would ne'er leave the castle. Of that I am certain."

"What of...what of the wing where you..." Alessandro hesitated.

That cemented her resolve. "The wing where you so eloquently related your reluctance in marrying a woman who could cause an avalanche?" she supplied. *Oui,* once more she garnered control of her wayward emotions. *Thankfully.*

There was a certain amount of pleasure in his wince. He cleared his throat. "*Si.*"

"Excellent, my lord," she said briskly, jumping to her feet. Somewhere along the line her vexation towards him had dissipated, leaving her feeling vulnerable. Here he was, risking his neck—literally—for the heir to a foreign kingdom. She was sadly aware that her childish infatuation for him had morphed into full-blown love. And if they did not locate Edric soon, she feared she would find him hanging from the gallows.

But Edric's safety came first. There was still the outside chance that no one had conceived she was missing. Once Prince and Cinde realized that Alessandro and she were missing together, the Visconte Alessandro de Lecce would indeed find himself chained to a woman whose eyes fluttered so furiously they could cause an avalanche. The thought made her heart ache. "Come, I know a shortcut."

Chapter 29

NICCÒLO BARGED INTO Alessandro's chamber determined to make him understand that Lady Kendra was not the woman for Aless. He was much too old for her for one thing, though Niccòlo refused to look any deeper into why that bothered him. The door bounded against the wall, bringing Sabato scurrying from the sitting room, his appearance somewhat harried.

Niccòlo demanded, "Where is he, Sabato?"

Aless seemed to be hiding from him. Terrified, more like, that his younger sibling would—*could*—thrash him silly. His aging brother surely found the competition intimidating. The thought filled Niccòlo with satisfaction. Niccòlo stood amid the opulent chamber wondering where to search next.

"Where is who?" Despite his appearance, his tone remained undaunted. The man was a statue.

"My beloved brother, who else?"

"He is not here?" Sabato lifted a brow.

"Enough with the theatrics, *per favore*," he said. "Tell me now."

"What is the problem, child?"

"*Child*?" Niccòlo bit out. He could barely speak for his teeth grinding together. It was a wonder they did not crumble under the pressure. Niccòlo pulled himself up to his full height, towering a good foot over the aging valet, folded his arms across his chest. "What are you hiding, old man?"

Before Sabato could answer a short knock sounded. Niccòlo spun for the door that still stood wide open. A servant cowered before him holding a silver tray.

"*Sì?*"

"A...a missive for...for Signore de Lecce."

Niccòlo snatched it up and slammed the door. In swift efficiency he sliced it open with an index finger.

"Niccòlo, I insist you not read your brother's private correspondence." Sabato actually snarled at him. It was too late, however, as Niccòlo had already determined the gist of the note. He looked up slowly; met Sabato's pained expression, shook the velum he held toward the old man.

"So, 'tis true? Padre was exiled from Spain many years ago? We are not of Italian nobility?"

The old man compressed his lips into a thin line.

"Tell me, Sabato," Niccòlo said more gently. "Where is Aless?"

"I do not know." Distress finally won out through Sabato's wringing his hands. "There are rumors he was thrown within the dungeon. But for all my efforts I have failed to locate him."

"What do you mean failed to locate him?" Niccòlo stopped, arm dropping to his side as Sabato's words slowly sunk in. "The dungeon? Who dared throw my brother in the dungeon?"

"Incredibly as it seems, talk is he'd kidnapped the heir apparent, and held him in the forest," the old man said, grasping his chest. "That fool, Arnald, the prince's cousin, clapped him in chains and threw away the key." Sabato's dramatics withstanding, this was a serious charge, sending a chill down Niccòlo's spine".

"*Dio!*" Niccòlo whispered. He refolded the missive and shoved it into his waistcoat. "I must find him. Where is Padre?"

"Bah, that *idiota*. Charming that witch of a woman, I fear."

"Lady Roche?" Niccòlo was aghast. That's all they needed— Papa fawning over the worst gossip in the palace. "I must find Aless. The dungeon, you say?"

"*Sí*. But how shall you find him?"

Niccòlo wore a path through the rich carpet. *How indeed?* There would be guards, keys that needed confiscating. Hell, they may all lose their heads.

Another soft rap sounded. Sabato reached it before Niccòlo and opened it, revealing a scowling Joseph Pinetti. He stood with one fist paused mid-air as if preparing to knock the heavy wood down barehanded.

His dark shrewd gaze took in their surroundings. "Where is Alessandro?" he asked quietly.

Though Sabato stood chest high and wispy-thin to Pinetti's broad build, Niccòlo felt his lips twitch when the valet jerked Joseph quite forcefully into the room, clapping the door closed behind him.

Niccòlo's words came out on a strangled laugh. "'Tis a good question."

Joseph's gaze shifted between him and Sabato. Finally coming to some internal decision, said, "I realize this may sound odd." Joseph's voice lowered even more so, as if he suspected ears resided in the walls, eyes piercing through the artwork. "I've had a vision."

"A vision?" With a lifted brow, Niccòlo parroted him, flatly.

Heavy brows beneath an intense scrutiny leveled a potent focus on Niccòlo. "I assure you 'tis not a matter to be taken lightly."

Niccòlo coughed into his hand. "Of course not, but I've no understanding of what you speak. A vision of what?" He could feel Sabato moving to stand behind him. The look in Joseph's eyes turned humorous, resting just past Niccòlo's shoulder.

"Alessandro's whereabouts," Joseph said. "I shall accompany you."

"No!" Sabato said. "You will stay available, Joseph. They are certain to come calling with questions. Someone must be about to answer—convincingly."

Niccòlo spun around quickly, scowling at Sabato. He glanced back at Joseph who wore a smirk. Unfortunately, it made perfect sense. "Where shall I find him?"

Chapter 30

HILDA SUCKED IN A furious breath, pressed the heel of her palm to her forehead, and stalked the brick walkway. Something dire was amiss and not a soul was talking. Bah! Cinderella not only had stolen Esmeralda's rightful heritage, but now she dared keep Esmeralda's whereabouts from her. She ruined everything. *Everything!*

Now the hoyden had turned Pricilla—her darling, darling Pricilla from her. There must be some way to stop Cinderella. Why, they would...

"*Bonjour*, Madame. You look especially troubled today. Tell me, *per favore,* there is something of which I may assist you?" The touch on Hilda's elbow was not unfamiliar, and not unwelcome. His timing could not have been more happenchance.

She gained control of her ire as a plan rippled through the deep recesses of her mind, surging their way forward as she cast the Conte de Lecce a brilliant smile.

"*SIGNORE*, WE HAVE MUCH to discuss, my dear sir."

"We do?" The Conte de Lecce, startled for a moment at the reception he'd received, lifted a brow.

"*Mais oui.*" Lady Roche attached herself to his arm in a solid grasp. He doubted a prying bar of iron could have forced her release. "A stroll through the gardens, perhaps, *Signore*?"

"My pleasure, my lady." He led her to the terrace doors and swung them open. A brisk wind whipped across his face. "After you, Madame," he bowed.

"*Merci, Signore.*"

He ushered the robust matron down stone steps and onto a weathered path strewn with fallen leaves. Truly, there was magic in the air, he thought. He could not keep the grin from his face. They sauntered along the path, the silence between them companionable. He was in no hurry after all, savoring the thrill that soon all that the eye could see would soon belong to him.

"I understand you have big plans, *Signore.*"

Her throaty voice broke into his musings. "*Perdono?*" A chill crept up his spine and he turned a critical eye on her. Jewels and fine silks did not conceal her colossal jowls, or soften the harsh venom that spewed from her mouth. She was a truly hateful woman. Expunging the woman might have him hailed as a hero. He sighed. It might also upset his plans greatly. He would savor a more fitting annihilation for her once he gained power.

She lifted one hefty shoulder. "There is talk."

Pasqual fought to suppress even the fraction of emotion. "Talk?" he inquired, politely.

"*Oui.* Just idle innuendo mind you, but as you well know, such nonsense can be invariably...damaging." She gave him a feral smile. Hackles raised, he steered her along the manicured lane, procuring all of her attention so as not to frighten her.

He smiled certain it wielded the same charm as a witch holding out a poisoned apple from her claw-like fingers. "Ah, perhaps you would not mind sharing these innuendos?" He increased their pace, worried some unfortunate would overhear. The passageway, marked with squared-stones, routed expertly through a portion of the forest. It suited his purposes. Mayhap her decimation was pre-destined.

"I am sure it is nothing, *Signore.*" Lady Roche gave him coquettish smile. On her massive features it appeared similar to one of those repulsive dog-breeds from China with the smashed in noses.

The significance of her smug references made him desperate to find out exactly what she inferred. He waited politely. He dare not reveal how desperate he needed her knowledge. He didn't have to wait long.

"An undercurrent talk of a coup seems to have taken hold."

The crash of Pasqual's carefully laid plans of the last ten years of his life flashed before his eyes. A sickness gripped his gut that threatened to bend him at the waist. Black speckles danced before him as he struggled for breath. The clutch she had on his arm suddenly lessened and he panicked.

"A coup?" he choked out. "Who would spout such nonsense?"

"Why, I believe I heard your own son speaking of it."

"*Dios,* you lie," he sputtered. All plans for her carefully constructed demise escaped his sense. His hand went to her meaty throat and he squeezed. A second later she dropped in mountainous heap. Oxygen filled his lungs, the black dots dispersed, leaving his vision and mind suddenly cleared. Calm settled over him until he glanced down at her unconscious figure.

Disgust filled him. Could she not have provoked him ten steps further along? Now he would have to drag her gargantuan form inside the trees. He squatted and put his fingertips to her neck. Her careless words had signed her own death warrant. 'Twould be no great loss, he grimaced wryly. *Si,* he'd probably would be hailed a hero.

"—they're quite rare."

"*Oui*, but luck will surely follow should we happen upon one."

Pasqual froze as light, amused feminine voices pierced his concentration. There was no time to finish off the hag. Leaves crunched with the moving footsteps. He leaped over his victim and darted within the shelter of the trees.

Chapter 31

"HOW FAR DOES THIS deserted portion of the castle extend?" Aless growled. He'd been following Esmeralda's lithe form for thirty minutes of the last hour. Endless, darkened, unpopulated corridors swallowed them. The castle was massive. 'Twas of no wonder mischief could abound. "Are you certain you know where you are going?"

"I play seek-and-hide with an inventive child of four; of course, I know where I am going."

His stomach let out a tumultuous roar. Quite embarrassing, but a man needed sustenance. A muffled giggled escaped his companion.

"You do not require nourishment?"

"I am a woman, *Signore*. We eat very little. Besides, 'tis highly improper for a woman to emit such bodily noises," she said, primly.

"Trousers, however, are an exception, I take it."

"Well, I could hardly climb out of the window in a full skirt and petticoats, could I?"

"*You climbed out the window*?" His voice echoed against the walls. Lowering it, he snatched her arm, capturing her gaze. "*Dio*. You little fool; you might have broken your graceful little neck."

"Quit manhandling me or I shall have to resort to other tactics again." She jerked her arm from him and stalked on. "Bad luck for you, *Signore*. As here I stand, leading you from certain disaster in that deathtrap of a cell in which Arnald had you stashed."

"Mm. And leading *yourself* into ruination."

She stopped so suddenly, he bumped into her. He'd only admired how fitted the form-fitting trousers were at this point, but without the petticoats and skirts of two stone, he suddenly felt the loss of that protection.

"Do not even speak to me of such a thing," she hissed.

He smiled at the irritation on her pert, heart-shaped face. He leaned in, touched his nose to hers. "Any reason why I should not?" Her lips were enticingly near.

"Need I remind you of your true feelings, *Signore*? Words spoken not far from where we now stand." Angry pointed breaths touched his lips with each uttered sound.

"My apologies, *Signorina*," he whispered.

"You've already apologized. Several times over." She sounded genuinely surprised.

"Not for that."

"Then wh—"

Alessandro seized her lips to his, effectively cutting her off. Shock rendered her immobile, and he took full advantage, cur that he was, coaxing her response. It started out subtle enough, but he soon turned hungry, urgent. It occurred to him she should feel insulted. Instead, only mere seconds passed before her arms twined about his neck, tugging him closer. The sensation left him light-headed and dizzy. He dragged his lips from her with ragged breaths heaving through his chest.

A smug satisfaction slowly filled him, he grinned against her lips. Surely, she must see their need to marry. He leaned back slowly, looked into her face. Her eyes were still closed. He gazed upon the thickest lashes. Awed by the beauty resting against her cheeks, her lips parted where her small rapid breaths escaped. Aless doubted anyone had been allowed near enough to witness such splendor. His chuckle burst through.

'Twas then it hit him! In a strange twist of fate, her batting eyes had saved her for *him*.

As if reading his thoughts, her eyes fluttered open in a startled glance. At once, the surge of wind pricked the air. "Shush," he whispered. He pushed his fingers through her hair, knocking the silly knitted cap from her head, reveled in the soft curls. He rested his lips on her forehead. The expulsion of her breath heated his chin. Her thick lashes tickled his cheeks, rendering a new resolve. A match with the anomalous Lady Esmeralda would be more any man could dream. That she loved children was obvious. The fiery temperament would never allow a life of anything so mundane. Who could ask more?

Then sensibility emerged. Yet, did he have a home in which to take her? If he was of Spanish descent as the Conte professed, Prince Charming and his kingdom were arch enemies of a century plus.

She swallowed and after a difficult moment, a grim smile touched her lips. "This is highly improper, *Signore.*"

"*Si, Signorina*...Essie," he could not resist adding. He had to wonder when he confessed his father's deception—his uncertain heritage, Would turn to one of loathing and disgust; or one that cowered in fear? He shifted his body, setting her firmly apart.

Her eyes narrowed on him, suspicion registering, hands fisting at her sides.

"Essie—Lady Esmeralda, I've much to confess..." he said softly.

"Confess?" she said sharply. She tossed her head. Fury rose from her like sparks spewing from the mouth of a volcano.

Aless had a lucid vision of how the rupture of Vesuvius pulverized an entire civilization. He wanted to draw from that heat, revel in her attentions. He took her fisted hands into his. Despite their tensed clenching, he could feel her vulnerability through a tremble she could not hide.

"Essie," he whispered, tugging her close. "I fear I've been misleading you—"

She jerked her hands from his. "Do not fret, *Signore.* I need no confessions from *you.* If you recall, I've already heard your *confessions, oui*?" she bit out angrily.

His own anger surged and he snagged her by her upper arms, torn by his desire to throttle her or to kiss more sense into her. "You know nothing!" How could she not read his crazed hunger for her, this avid need for her? It squeezed his heart like a manacle of steel, making it difficult for him to draw in oxygen. "*Dio!* How can you not—" He couldn't finish, he was so angry. He fitted his mouth over hers and kissed her until...until...soft bickering seeped through to his consciousness. Slow, like molasses, but heavy and...there.

He'd lost his mind. Most definitely, he was the elder son of the Conte. Aless moved his mouth to her ear. "*Tesoruccio*, listen." A sense of reprieve filled him.

The sudden tenseness in her stance indicated his words unnecessary. She nodded, fear filling her eyes.

Dio! They were planning an attack during the Coronation Ceremony. Did she understand the language? What they proposed?

Her copper tresses spilled through his fingers like spun silk, so it was with great effort he turned his attention back to the reigning issue and forced himself away. Confusion drew her brows together. He ached to kiss away every uncertainty, but his father's voice blaring about them jarred them into reality.

Whether or not she would have him, he silently vowed her safety.

HIS ANGER WAS PALPABLE, rolling off him in waves. He did not kiss like he did not want her. But how could he be angry at her for *that*? She was not the one who'd professed aversion of marriage to an unsuitable candidate.

Blast him. She'd admired him for years. Years! And for what? To be held in such low regard? Yet, his lips fit hers with such perfection—such adulation. Confusion filled her. She thought his fingers trembled in her hair. She studied his expression. Gone was the anger, or sign of any previous tenderness. It yielded nothing but implacable blankness. Gone, save the lightness of his touch. He leaned in. "Where is your hat?" he whispered against her ear. She hadn't even noticed it missing. He leaned down and swept it up from the floor—placed it squarely on her head.

Rapid fire Spanish echoed softly about, and was difficult to follow. The few words that penetrated her kiss-fogged brain made her stiffen. "That sounds like your father," she whispered to Alessandro.

"*Si*," he agreed, sharply. He placed a finger against her lips, effectively shushing her.

"He warns them against killing him," she said. Relief hit her knees first and she sagged against the wall. She caught little else.

"*Si.*"

Irritation at his parroting replies had her snapping, "What is it, *Signore*?"

Rather than answer, he addressed her with that steady unyielding gaze, the intensity beneath, however, frightened her. "If you have some idea of

Prince Edric's whereabouts, my lady, now would be the time to disclose them." His pitch was low, cold, controlled. She'd never seen this side of Alessandro de Lecce. His formal title of Visconte suddenly suited him.

Unable to quell the quiver that threatened her ability to stand, she watched him with unblinking eyes, trying to decipher his demeanor. 'Twas the urgency that squeezed her heart. She inhaled deeply. "*Certainement,*" she said. "Follow me." She spun on her heel.

Keeping to the shadows, Essie winded her way further into the depths of castle, impossibly aware of Alessandro on her heels. They'd already searched many of Edric's favorite haunts. But she knew one or two more. The corridor shifted into dankness due to the absence of daily activity, stirring the dust beneath their feet. Cobwebs swung like ghostly tendrils reaching toward them, swayed by a light breeze not of her doing. The difference in temperature that touched Essie's head versus her fingers was remarkable.

It was easy to forget some of the castle's disintegrating portions when one's feet were sunk deep in luxurious Aubusson rugs and set off by warm lantern lamps. She shuddered at her morbid thoughts, staying close to the stone walls as a guide.

These parts of the palace, so uninhabitable and isolated, were precisely what raised Essie's concerns. A child of four had no such cares. Everything and everywhere became a quest for adventure or its own vaulted cloister. Worry had her sprinting through the dark, but Alessandro's grip held her from running full out.

"Watch the debris," he said, kicking a piece of broken wood from their path. "All I need for the noose to tighten round my neck is for you to break yours."

"Your concern is touching," she muttered. She pulled her arm from his grasp determined forward, lest she faint on the spot. The only way to ward off the fear was to keep moving.

The corner they rounded indicated they'd reached the west tower. Ahead were the steps she sought, the railing had long since disintegrated, if, in fact, it had ever sported one. Essie climbed without care. If Edric had run from villains, this would be his destination. Her apprehension lay in his lack of escape were he followed. She stumbled. In her haste she'd almost forgotten her companion, until the sinew of iron muscle caught her by the waist.

"Have a care, Essie."

Essie took small comfort in his deep resonance, the warmth of his arm, the flutter of air brushing her nape. Once this adventure ended she would never feel the heat of his kiss, the strength of his hold. She breached the top of the second flight, breathless.

"I see your friend, Joseph Pinetti's visions are interestingly accurate."

She gasped at the familiar, but not unfriendly voice. She stopped so suddenly, Alessandro had to shift the two of them quickly from the edge of the treacherous staircase lest they fall back from whence they came.

"Niccòlo, what the devil," Alessandro hissed.

"We must talk, *fratello*."

"Sorry, *fratello*, now is not the time." Alessandro bit out.

Essie stepped beyond Alessandro's reach, her gaze moving between them.

"I'm afraid I must insist." There was a hardness to Alessandro's younger brother's tone, so unlike him, that frightened her. "Some information has come to my attention that cannot be ignored."

"Really, Niccòlo?" Sarcasm dripped from Alessandro.

Any other time, the smirk Niccòlo handed Alessandro would have had Essie laughing outright, but now all she felt was panic. Hand at her throat, her pulse beat a riff of rapid staccato notes that would do Mozart proud. She narrowed her eyes on Niccòlo. "What do you mean regarding Monsieur Pinetti's visions?"

Neither one answered. In fact, they sizing up one another as intently as if they were gladiators from ancient Rome. There weren't quite circling, but 'twasn't far behind.

Mon...Dieu! If Niccòlo could find them, who was next? They could stand there and bicker until the cow jumped the moon for all she cared. Essie turned, but only managed one step before the steel band of hard muscle grasped her once more about the waist.

"One moment, my lady." Alessandro's cold narrowed eyes were on his brother but his words brooked no argument. She tried pushing his arm away, to no avail.

Niccòlo's gaze widened slightly scrutinizing her unconventional attire. Then an unsuccessful attempt to hide the twitch of his lips had her cheeks warming. "New evening wear, Lady Esmeralda?" he shot in her direction.

"Day gown," she murmured, finally managing to shove Alessandro's arm away.

"Lovely."

"Get to it, Niccòlo. We are in a hurry."

Essie resisted the urge to squirm under Niccòlo's assessing glance. He turned back to his brother. "There are rumors."

Alessandro quirked a brow in her direction, before giving his attention back to Niccòlo. "How shocking."

"I would not be so glib, were I you." Niccòlo's face flushed darkly.

"A good point," he muttered.

"Speak plainly, *Signore*," Essie said, sharply.

Panic touched his features. "May I, Aless?"

Alessandro lifted a shoulder in acquiescence. Essie's lips tightened at Niccòlo's request to Alessandro rather than her. But she waited in agitated silence.

"They say you were thrown in the dungeon." He glanced between the two of them.

Essie shrugged at that. It was true, what could she say?

"That you had the heir apparent in the forest."

Also, true, but that she refused to acknowledge. Gossip was the fodder of castle life, after all.

"Anything else?" Alessandro said, blandly. She wondered how he managed that air of blatant disinterest. 'Twas a neat trick. Most especially when one's eyes did not give away one's every thought.

"That Sir Arnald clapped you in chains and threw away the key."

"The keys were hanging next to the door," Essie said.

"*You* let him out?" Niccòlo gaped at her.

A wicked grin touched Alessandro's lips. "She escaped through a window."

"*Dio,* do you not understand? This is not a game." Niccòlo leaned in so quickly, hovered so tall, it caught her unaware. Her eyes started to flutter, voice failing her.

But Alessandro, quickly, moved between them, shielding her from his brother's efforts to intimidate. Alessandro shoved Niccòlo, forcing him to stumble back. Essie edged her way to the door. She turned back to see Alessandro's measured gaze on his brother. Matching the venom in his tone, he said softly, "Do not think to threaten Lady Esmeralda, Niccòlo. If you've nothing further, we must be on our way."

"*Uno momento*, Aless." Niccòlo reached into his coat and withdrew a shaft of expensive stationery.

Alessandro snatched it from Niccòlo and snapped it open. A sharp grimace of...pain?—touched his expression, but quickly disappeared. He refolded the missive, and stashed it into his own shirt. The tension in the abandoned hall grew tenfold. Whatever news Niccòlo brought, she feared the brothers would come to blows.

Essie, having managed control of her senses once more, digested the scene before her, and considered Niccòlo carefully. Whatever their differences, there was also a sudden understanding between the two. She had excellent instincts. Look how her friendship with Cinde turned out, after all. She sucked in a deep breath. "Edric is missing," she blurted.

"*Missing*! There was nothing said about Prince Edric missing," Niccòlo frowned.

A rush of air left her body. "That is a relief," she said. "Perhaps it has bought us time."

"You, perhaps. Me, they will string up by my—"

"Aless!" Niccòlo snapped.

She hoped her blush was not as red as a blacksmith's iron fresh from the fire. Niccòlo's face certainly was. "We've not much time. Come, the hour grows late." Essie swept from the chamber, leaving Alessandro and Niccòlo to follow.

Niccòlo was now party to their rescue efforts, whether Alessandro approved or not. Regardless, the help was welcome.

Chapter 32

DESPITE THEIR IMPENDING danger, Alessandro could not restrain a grin at Essie's retreating figure. She looked ridiculous with her copper locks poking out from the ugly cap in such haphazard fashion. The term 'fashion' used loosely in this context, he thought, eyeing the fitted trousers. Dirt streaked her cheeks that had him clenching his fists in an effort to keep his hands to himself. He was captivated. He supposed fitted trousers would ne'er become the norm for young women bent on unprecedented escapades. A shame, that.

"Lady Esmeralda, slow down, *per favore*," Aless commanded.

Of course, she acted as if he hadn't said a word, plowing ahead. He let out a snort and picked up his pace. Ignoring Niccòlo's muffled curse, he shoved his brother aside to reach her. 'Twas not like he hadn't the urge to add a few inappropriate words of his own. She stomped ahead, escaped curls bouncing beneath the ridiculous hat. Arms bent at the elbow, lent a determined velocity to her gait.

He snagged her by an arm. "At the risk of repeating myself, *Essie*, please slow. We need a stratagem." When her stubborn huff met his ears, he pulled her to an unceremonious halt. "*For the safety of the child.*"

The magic words. They worked. She jerked her arm from his grasp. "I'm listening." Fire flashed in her eyes, chest rising with her rapid breath. His eyes landed at the flickering throb on her neck.

Alessandro tugged at the shirt collar suddenly choking him, blatantly aware of his younger brother's rapt attention.

"*Essie*?" Niccòlo choked out. "That's much too familiar, Aless."

"A term of endearment," Alessandro said, eyes never straying from the erratic palpitation that gave away his intended's anxiety. "What do you propose we do if—*when* we locate him?"

"We shall have to conceal him. There are several outlying cottages. Caves." It was panic speaking. The proof was in the flutter of her lashes. With each uttered word, the flurry became more pronounced.

"And how do you propose we get to these outlying cottages or caves?" he asked, calmly.

"...h-horses," she whispered.

"We cannot run, my lady." Aless took her hand in his. The soft, smooth texture reminded him he stood with the future queen's sister.

She glanced down at their juncture. "*Non*, I-I suppose not."

"You shall take him to his mother, *sí?* She will be beside herself with worry."

"Does she just meander in with the child, Aless? That does not seem so wise," Niccòlo said.

"Lady Esmeralda needs an escort, Niccòlo," Alessandro said pointedly.

"Aless—" Niccòlo started, objection written in every line of his face.

"If they find me they will chain me to the wall." It grated on Aless to ask, but he had no choice. "*Per favore, fratello.*"

True to the brothers they were, Niccòlo's head bobbed a sharp nod, his pause barely discernable.

"But what of you, my lord? They will think...think..."

"We must think of Prince Edric, my lady."

The stubborn resolve in her eyes softened at the significance of his words. Aless watched Essie, fascinated by the thoughts so plainly crossing her expression.

She tapped her chin with a trembling forefinger. "It might not be so difficult," she said. "There is a scavenger hunt this afternoon. I shall win, of course," she grimaced. "I have the ultimate prize."

"*Sì*," Niccòlo said. "*If* he is located."

She faced Aless with a direct, troubled look. The depths of her concern stirred in him a sudden need to protect. "What of you?" she asked.

He said, "You are a woman not simply swayed, *no*?" The tone came out abrasive and harsh. "I will deal with the Conte." He took one arm and turned her gently. "We've wasted enough time. Lead the way, my lady. Where shall we find him?"

Her gaze moved over her shoulder between him and Niccòlo, after a moment she squared her shoulders, raised her chin and slipped through an open door, he and Niccòlo close behind. "There," she whispered. "Look."

A bundle of old drapes lay piled in a corner. It took a moment before Aless spotted their quarry. He had to squint to make out the young prince, so well he blended in the folds. Cherub cheeks streaked with dust; dark curls matted, he otherwise appeared astonishingly unharmed...and sleeping soundly. A relief so great filled Aless, he had to blink back a suspicious sting in his eye. He blew out a stunned breath.

Now, to somehow return the precocious little prince without getting, he, his brother, or future wife—flogged.

"You must hurry, Niccòlo," Aless said. "If you are seen, Lady Esmeralda, I fear your unusual attire will create a maelstrom of pandemonium." *With Lady Roche leading the charge.*

"THE LITTLE PRINCE SLEEPS like a hibernating bear, *no*?" Niccòlo said.

Essie giggled, if somewhat hysterically, as relief seeped through her tense muscles. Edric still slumbered draped over Niccòlo's shoulder like a sack of onions. Soon he would be in safe hands, the danger turned over to his father to lead the charge against this unknown battle. "*Certainement*, he always has. He is heavy too." She glanced behind her.

Niccòlo flashed her quick smile, and she was struck by the similarities between the brothers. "I assure you I can handle the load."

Essie led Niccòlo quietly through the dusty corridors, closer to safety.

"Who do you suppose they are? How can they speak so...so coldly of...of stealing a child?" A shudder rippled across her skin.

"Someone spoke of stealing the prince?" Shock colored his tone and she realized he hadn't known.

"I...I heard them. Late yesterday..."

"'Tis why you were hiding in the forest, *no*?" he said, softly.

"*Mais oui*," she whispered.

"And Aless?"

"He saw us and followed. We waited hours before we were certain they'd gone. By then, I fear, the hounds had been set loose. And, well, you know the rest. They clapped Alessandro in chains and set aside the key."

"But not so far from your reach, did they, my lady?" His statement was rhetorical. He shook his head as if he couldn't believe the direction events had taken. "Regardless, the safety of the child is imperative. I can only hope we do not lose our heads over this."

On this she could reassure him. "You worry far too much. We've a fairy godmother about."

"A fairy godmother," he snorted. "What nonsense is this?"

"Is Edric still sleeping?" she called softly over her shoulder. "We've never mentioned Fairy Godmother to him."

"*Sí*, he is still sleeping. How much further?"

"Not far." She grinned. Apparently, Niccòlo was not impressed with her divulgence. To an outsider it might seem a bit fantastic, she supposed. She hurried along the corridor listening for any miniscule of sound. Silence relieved her mind—silence assured their anonymity.

"Hold," Niccòlo said, softly.

"What is it?"

"Maman?" Edric whimpered.

"Oh, Edric, darling." Essie spun, reaching for her nephew. "Don't be scared. You know Signore de Lecce."

"*Non*, 'tis not the *Signore*," Edric wriggled in his arms, frantic to get away.

"This is Niccòlo, *ma chère*, Signore Alessandro's brother."

Niccòlo gently lowered Edric to his feet then moved aside. She had ne'er been so happy to see her nephew's little face. He looked so innocent.

"I am pleased to make your acquaintance, Your Highness." Niccòlo offered him a formal bow.

"Aunt Sessie?"

"*Oui.*" She started when Edric's small body bounded into her chest for a tight hug.

He clung, bringing a piercing sting to her eyes. She dropped to her knees and set him on his feet but he refused to relinquish his hold.

"I waked-ed up, Aunt Sessie." He buried his nose in the crook of her neck, voice muffled. "I heard voices so I hided. But they didn't find me, Aunt Sessie. I-I waited til they left then I went in the special place we talked 'bout. I knew you would find me. You're the *bestest* seeker." His scant body quivered against hers, and she clung to him just as tightly.

"That's high praise, indeed," she said on a breath of panic. *They came into his room?* She bit back bile. "Edric, darling." Essie pulled him away. "Listen to me, *s'il vous plaît*. We must sneak back. No one must know we've been hiding. Can you do that, my little prince?"

He threw his tiny arms about her neck. "*Mais oui*, Aunt Sessie. I want my Maman."

She blinked back more tears. He trembled in her embrace. "You're safe now," she whispered. She stood on shaky legs. There was no time to lose.

"What are you wearing, Aunt Sessie?" Edric squeaked.

It was followed quickly by Niccòlo's sharp gasp of pain.

"*Si, Signorina*. What *are* you wearing? 'Tis unusual and enticing, indeed." The unfamiliar voice startled a sharp scream from her.

Essie's heart dropped, her eyes flittered—'twas not Alessandro's lyrical resonance addressing her from behind. Time froze as if encased by a small globe filled with snow. A glint of steel registered on her senses, attached to a beefy arm marred with...with strange emblems. She'd never seen the like. They looked like markings she'd read about. Rituals that took place in less civilized cultures. Or...or pirates.

She must remain calm. "Run, Edric," she said softly. "Do you understand?"

"The child will be going nowhere, my lady." The body attached to the deadly voice advanced. Light glinted off a steel blade he welded. She backed away, her gaze mesmerized.

Where was Niccòlo? Why did he not step forward? She spun. She opened her mouth to scream, horrified by the sight that met her—Niccòlo in a bloodied heap.

"*Now*, Edric. *Go!*" she screamed. Edric ran.

She gasped for air. So much blood. He was dead. Dead.

"*Dio!* You shall pay for that, my lady."

'Twas the last thing she heard. All else faded with a sharp pain that landed against her temple. Succumbing to the blackness claiming her, she uttered one prayer.

That Edric made it to safety.

ALESS PROWLED THE TOWER in a restless pace. Niccòlo should have been back ten minutes ago. Blast him. How difficult was it to escort a gentle woman and a small child to safety? Of course, said 'gentle woman' was sporting men's pants and the small child happened to be heir to the Chalmers throne. He paused before a grimy window where angry waves of the sea crashed mercilessly against jagged rocks.

"Damnation," he whispered. Fear gripped Aless by the throat, and refused to let go. How long must he wait? Mayhap Joseph was not the only clairvoyant one.

Dio! He'd waited ten minutes too long, for certain. The issue now came in determining how to find his brother. He kept close to the wall, making his way down the treacherous stairs. It chilled him to the bone, thinking of the young prince running loose amid such hazards. Once Aless reached the main level, he listened intently for the sound of foreign tongues. How fortunate training the war had in teaching him to move well in silence.

Father or no, the *bastardos* would be dead before they realized what hit them if he found them first.

A muted groan touched his ears. All his senses shifted into a singular focus. His fingertips tingled, the skin along his nape prickled.

"Take that message to your *fratello*." A voice full of fury spewed, yet Aless discerned pain washing through.

He broke into a run.

Too, late. The hall was deserted but for a mass of—

"Niccòlo?" The surge of suffocating panic seared him. He dropped to one knee and pressed two fingers to his brother's neck. The beat of his pulse was strong and Aless let out a rush of air. Alive, thank God. He'd almost tripped over him, slipped in a slick pool covering the stone floor. Only the dust gave him traction. "Can you hear me?"

"Aless? *Sì.*" His gasp was raspy.

He slipped an arm about Niccòlo's shoulders, and assisted him to sitting. Blood gushed from a rip in his shirt where Niccòlo's arm met his chest. Dangerously close to his heart. Panic fueled fear by raged through him.

The shreds looked skillfully placed with the sharp thin tip of a blade. The cut appeared clean, not deep. A warning? Tugging a handkerchief from his shirt, Aless pressed it to the wound. "What happened? The child?" Aless demanded softly.

"He...he got away." Niccòlo put a hand to his head and winced. Niccòlo favored his left arm, and a protruding lump on his hard head had already begun to form.

"Lady Esmeralda...?" *Of course she had*, though a knot twisted deep within his belly.

"I'm afraid not. They spared me with a kick to the head to deliver their message."

"And a sliced up shoulder," Aless growled. Fury ceased him with a force so blinding, spots danced before his eyes. He had to inhale slowly before he could choke out the words through the lump in his throat. "Was there more than one?"

"No. Leastways, I only heard one voice."

"Who was he? Did you recognize him? Tell me, Niccòlo, word for word, what was the message?"

"If you wish to see her unharmed, you will let matters lie. *Mi dispiace,* Aless. I'm sorry. It is inexcusable, I know. I was caught by surprise," he grimaced.

Aless ached to lay blame at the feet of his brother, but Niccòlo had not been to war. This burden fell upon his own head and he carried full responsibility for Essie—Lady Esmeralda. If he did not keep her from harm, then he deserved the full brunt of the consequences. "Enough, Niccòlo. We must tend to your wound. The fault is mine. Arguing over it is a waste of time."

Just beyond Niccòlo's bloodied shoulder he spotted it. The ridiculous knitted cap Essie had worn to hide her lustrous dark red curls. Aless assisted Niccòlo to his feet, then swooped it off the ground. "Come," he growled.

Someone would die—by his hand, he vowed.

Chapter 33

HEART POUNDING, EDRIC RAN as fast as he could and rounded a corner. He must find another place to hide, someplace they would ne'er find him. He would succeed, he told himself, *he* was a *good* hider.

Edric darted into the second empty chamber. The seeker always looked in the first one.

It was hard to think but he must, Aunt Sessie needed him. Heavy footsteps echoed against the stones making it hard to tell how close the mean man was. He smelled bad too, he thought, wrinkling his nose.

Pressing his lips together, he flattened himself close to the wall. That *stupide* man would not catch *him*! He knew secret places even Aunt Sessie did not know about. Edric slipped behind the door and waited. *What should he do?*

He closed his eyes, tight. *Think, think, think.*

Almost every chamber had another, less visible entrance for the servants. But that would not help Aunt Sessie. He peered through the crack. 'Twasn't long before the mean man stepped into sight. Edric covered his mouth with his hand, lest he make the slightest noise—Aunt Sessie was hanging over the man's shoulder. He was big—bigger and heavier than Papa. And his hands were putridly dirty. At least the one he could see, and there were odd drawings on his arm. He had lots of hair on his face too. He committed every detail to memory. Papa would want to know everything.

Suddenly, it struck him. He would follow the *stupide monsieur*. Find out where he was taking Aunt Sessie. Oh! Panic seized him. Papa was with the Spanish Prince. Wait. Uncle Arnald. *Oui!* Uncle Arnald was almost as strong as Papa. The scuffled footsteps paused, just inches from Edric's hidden place behind the door, right under his nose. The mean man smelled awful.

"Where are you, you little bugger!" His voice jarred Edric, made him want to run.

But he held his breath and pretended he and Aunt Sessie were playing, and pressed his back further against the wall. The stone was cold through his thin night rail, but Edric was determined. He would not fail Aunt Sessie.

He blinked back an unexpected prickling of tears and wished for Papa. Papa would kill the bad man. He was a great warrior. His Papa would soon be King!

Edric swallowed his tears and stiffened his spine. If only he were bigger. He would stab that man with his own sword.

A BLAZING FIRE IN the hearth with his princess at his side were all Prince ever desired. She settled him like no other. Her delicacy enchanted and touched him deep inside. He guided her through the door and saw her to a comfortable chair near the heat. Surprisingly, the library did not appear inundated with family members. Only his cousin and Lady Pricilla sat ensconced in a quiet corner, talking feverishly.

Arnald's frustration with Lady Pricilla was succinct, and Prince found it difficult to conceal his amusement. An expectant wife could drive the strongest man to his knees. And Arnald was halfway there. Neither one glanced their way.

Granted the chamber was large. The drapes billowed in soft waves from an open window. Lady Pricilla, it seemed, could not handle, with any certainty, stuffy air.

Prince moved near the fire and held out his hands. It had been a long and tiring night. Prince Reynaldo and Princess Isabella had insisted on their company for dinner that went long into the early morning. As an important alliance for Chalmers, he'd been obligated. And with his father's death, the change in the air was imminent.

Blessedly, the evening proved successful, and Prince felt confident he'd strengthened the ties. He glanced over at his wife. Quiet pride filled him knowing her serene presence had played such a vital role. "*Bonjour*, cousin. Lady Pricilla."

"Cill! Is something wrong?"

Lady Pricilla started at her sister's voice.

Normally Prince found Lady Pricilla's matter-of-fact, no-nonsense, pragmatic manner quite refreshing. This day however something set him on edge and he narrowed his eyes on her. His cousin and his wife were up to something. It was no secret all three sisters were somewhat mischievous. Marriage had not dulled their wit one bit. But what? His dread increased ten-fold when Arnald prowled across the room.

Lady Pricilla stood and followed quickly on his heels. "Must we?" Her soft question raised the hair on Prince's nape.

"I fear so." Arnald growled.

Prince felt a sudden urge to protect his princess and moved beside her.

"What is it?" Cinderella demanded, obviously tuned in to their tension. She started to rise, but Prince stayed her with a hand on her shoulder.

"You are troubled?" Prince demanded calmly.

"You could say that," Arnald said. "Late afternoon yesterday, you may have learned that—"

"—the archery tournament," Pricilla interrupted. "I won the archery tournament."

"You always win the archery tournament, Cill," Cinderella said, mildly.

Arnald glared at his wife. His *enceinte* wife. A most curious action from his doting cousin, Prince thought.

Lady Pricilla, then, in all theatricality placed the back of her hand against her eyes as if a pain in her head was about to make her swoon. "I fear I must lie down, Darling. I am not feeling so well."

Even more curious was Arnald's reaction given that he was set to sever anyone's head who happen to look crossways at her.

"Mayhap not, *ma chère*, but I'm sure my Maman will be more than delighted to offer a tonic for your ailment, *non*?" His tone challenged his wife.

Well, that was somewhat cold-blooded.

Lady Pricilla's head snapped up, her gaze panicked. In true character, however, Arnald grabbed her hand. The squeeze Prince detected in their clutched hands tightened something in his own heart. And when tears dampened Lady Pricilla's lashes, Prince had to fight a stir of trepidation. Lady Pricilla was not one prone to tears.

Prince leveled a hard stare on Arnald. "Mayhap you should leave all drama aside and tell us what is really going on."

Pricilla pulled her hand from Arnald's and rushed to Cinderella's side. "Oh, darling, I'm so sorry—"

"—Cill, whatever are you about—"

Arnald's pain-filled gaze seared Prince, his words punching him as soundly as an unprotected blow to his gut. "It's Edric—he's missing."

Chapter 34

THE GROAN THAT REACHED Essie's ears was painful. A soft mewling animalistic sound that came from her own lips.

"Ah, *Mademoiselle*, you return to the living, I see. The Conte will be pleased, *no*?"

The Conte? Alessandro wasn't the Conte, he was Visconte, the heir apparent. And what did he mean he would be pleased?

She must have hit her head because nothing made sense. Nothing looked familiar. Words she could barely comprehend heavily accented competed with the pounding in her head. And why was she laying flat on a concrete floor?

"Where is Alessandro? He's not the Conte, you know." She struggled to sit, if only to keep the cold stone from seeping through the thin cotton of her shirt, but she had trouble gathering her balance. "Who are you? *Where* are you?" With each word the realization of the situation seeped in. Her hands were bound. Tightly.

The room was shadowed, and her assailant's low maniacal laugh echoed off the stone walls.

Nothing in her sights clued her in to her location. Which was odd. She knew every inch of the castle, thanks to Edric. But then memory flooded her. "Edric!" she gasped. Visions of Niccòlo's blood and crumpled body stabbed through her mind with refreshing accuracy.

"He managed to escape. 'Tis the only reason you live, *Mademoiselle*. You see, we need your persuasive techniques in securing his capture."

"You shall have to kill me first," she growled.

"I am sure that can be arranged."

Alarm skittered over her skin. "And Niccòlo? Is he...is he...dead..." her voice trailed on a whisper.

Another crack of menacing laughter sounded. "*Non*, my sweet. He serves as our messenger."

If possible, her head pounded harder, her vision swayed. "I-I don't understand." She wriggled her wrists to no avail. The bindings were efficiently secured. Her feet, at least, were unbound, thank the heavens. She breathed in slow breaths, willed her eyes to adjust to the dimmed lighting. After a space of time, she was able to make out her captor situated deep in the shadows. He sat against the wall with his legs stretched out before him, crossed at the ankles, arms folded over his chest.

She caught the gleam of his rotted teeth and shuddered. The picture reminded her of the wolf in a recent tale she'd read by Charles Perrault, *Les Petit Chaperon Rouge*. The young, courteous, and well-bred girl had done herself no favor when having listened to a stranger. The reality was harsh when she'd been eaten by a wolf. Oh, why had she read such a horrid story? She preferred *agreeable* endings. Essie feared her ending might parallel that of that unfortunate girl.

She ground her teeth and grimaced. *Non.* The man was not a cannibal. Not if she had anything to say about it. Something caught her attention near the door but she dare not glance over outright. Her stomach dropped ten feet when she realized from her peripheral vision it was Edric.

Horrified, the monster would see him, she squeaked, "Sir? Mayhap I could use your assistance?"

"BLAST IT, ALESS. ARE YOU trying to finish off what the knife failed to yield?" Niccòlo hissed.

"*Scusa.*" Aless lightened his touch immediately. "We're going to need help, I fear."

"Who, *mio fratello*, my brother? 'Tis our own padre behind these nefarious plans from all I've gathered." He shook his head. "'Tis inconceivable."

Aless understood the sentiment all too well. "*Si,*" he agreed.

"If we approach anyone at his point, we shall most likely be considered in cahoots with the *bastardo.*"

"Then we shall have to choose our ally carefully." Aless taped the last of the bandage over Niccòlo's shoulder. "That should hold. Have Sabato give it a thorough cleansing. It's difficult to believe our own father would kill us. Perhaps that explains the neatly applied cut. You didn't recognize the assailant, perchance?"

"No. He was not as tall as you or I. Black hair, black eyes, though broad in build."

"The same as any other Spaniard or Italiano. It could not be easy, *no*?" Aless pushed away the knot of dread churning deep in his belly. Staying focused was the only way to help Essie—Lady Esmeralda. He refused to believe otherwise.

"I seem to recall odd markings on his arms."

"You mean indelible writings—on his skin?"

"*Sí,* though I didn't recognize the patterns."

"Then he should be easy enough to identify. There cannot be many around with those kinds of markings."

"You are in love with Lady Esmeralda, *no*? How shall we find her, Aless?"

Aless felt the iron bands tighten about his chest at Niccòlo's soft accusation then plea. He sounded the younger brother who looked up to him all those years ago. Aless focused his resolve and grasped Niccòlo's hand, no longer the hand of a child, but that of a man.

"First, we enlist the aid of Sabato. Success is within our grasp," he promised. "Or we die trying."

Chapter 35

"AND WHAT OF ESSIE?" Cinderella's voice shifted an entire octave. "Where is she?"

"She is missing, as well," Pricilla said. She went on to explain events from the night before. How Edric and Essie were found with Alessandro de Lecce at the edge of the forest. How her husband (thoughtlessly—though this she maintained silently) tossed him below stairs without the least scrap of an explanation. And how he'd banished to Essie to her chambers. Her escape. Her aid in releasing Alessandro.

"But...but..." Cinde sputtered, disbelieving. Pricilla couldn't blame her. The whole scenario was fraught with unanswered questions. "But how did she escape her rooms?"

Pricilla winced.

"Through a window," her husband so generously bit out.

"But we're two levels high!"

Pricilla pressed her lips together. She'd kill Essie with her own hands for this mess. On the flip side, however, her preoccupation with this turn of events had kept her wayward stomach from dominating her time and thoughts. She snuck a peek at Prince from the corner of her eye, and her ill-begotten stomach churned.

He stood tall and rigid. Most unyielding. As formidable as she'd ever remembered seeing him.

"We must find them." Cinde's voice bordered on hysterics. She threw off Prince's touch and rose.

Pricilla found her fingertips pressing to her midsection finally understanding what she'd thought she never would. Cinde's child might be lost to her. Her sister wasn't thinking of the heir to the throne, or the future king. She was frantic for her young son. Tears pricked the backs of Cill's eyes, and she blinked quickly. "But how?" Pricilla whispered. "It's been hours since we've discovered Essie and Alessandro missing." Again, she stole a look at Prince. His rage was so taut, she flinched.

He answered calmly. "We start with de Lecce's chambers. Not that we will succeed, but 'tis a starting place. Then we speak to the Conte and Niccòlo. We shall find him, my love." The softness so smooth, Pricilla found she was terrified.

Cinde paced the library like hunted prey.

Pricilla felt helpless. There were no words she could offer to reassure her sister. She shifted her attention to Arnald. She knew him well and the look on his expression could only be interpreted as calculating. "Mayhap, 'tis time to sound the alarm," Pricilla suggested.

Her husband's jaw was set, and she worried the direction his thoughts had taken. She glanced quickly at Prince and realized that whatever thoughts each harbored, they were one and the same. It could not bode well, more than likely spelling danger and closet discussions that did not include her and Cinde!

After an interminable silence Arnald finally spoke. "A word if you please, cousin?"

"*Certainement.*"

"*Non.*" Pricilla and Cinde's voices united.

Pricilla met her sister's eyes. Perhaps in this area she could help. "You will not exclude us from your discussions. We are women, true, but we also have brains, and believe it or not, common sense."

Cinde gathered herself with a poise that would serve her well as the queen she would soon become. Her voice showed none of the quaver previously heard. She gave a stately smile of which Pricilla knew she'd never be more proud.

"Cill is right." Cinde looked at Arnald then Prince. "I suspect you both believe this has something to do with the items discovered several years ago."

Pricilla could see right away Cinde had the right of it. Arnald's features went curiously blank. La! A sure sign.

"Papa." Edric burst through the door, breathless.

Pricilla thought her heart would stop in her chest.

"Edric! Son, where have you been?" Edric leaped into his arms.

"Papa, we...we have to s...save..." He huffed jagged breaths rushing to tell his tale. "...Aunt Ses...ses..sie. A big ug...ugly man has her." Prince met Arnald's eyes over his son's head.

"You are safe." Prince enveloped his son in a hug so fierce, he was hidden from view.

Cinde rushed over to do the same, but Edric wriggled free, having none of it. Her eyes glittered with unshed tears, yet she said nothing.

"Papa, there is no time, *s'il vous plaît*." The gravity of the situation had his small voice cracking in an effort to hold back his tears. "We must save her. You have to kill the mean man."

"Where did you see her, son?" Arnald said. The urgency in his tone had Pricilla raising from the settee and going to Cinde. She took her hand. Their husbands would need the little prince's assistance, and Cinde would have to let him go—a most difficult feat.

Edric's small chest puffed out. "I shall take you to her."

"Edric—"

"We haven't a choice, Cousin," Arnald said, softly. "Time is critical."

Prince winced, glancing at Cinde. Pricilla felt Cinde's shudder of realization as the same sense of helplessness spread through her own limbs.

"Your Maman will fell me with a single blow should so much as a strand of hair is harmed on your head." The words poured from him and his gaze never strayed from his wife.

"She needs me, Papa. I have to save her." Pricilla knew the little solider was too young to fight but did not quite comprehend the fact. Ironically, he was the only one who could help.

"What of Signore de Lecce, Edric?" Arnald asked him.

"The mean man stabbed him, then kicked him. I fear he is dead."

"*Dead!*" The countenance of Pricilla's uneasy stomach, roiled in protest. "Find Essie, now," Pricilla demanded.

Prince grimaced. "Show us where, son. Can you do that?" Prince pulled on the bell chord, and a servant entered. "Send for the head guard, *vite.*"

Chapter 36

"I HAVE A PLAN. If we can manage to pull it off without getting our heads blown off 'twill be a miracle. But 'tis worth a shot." Aless paused before a window overlooking the crashing waves.

"'Tis better than sitting around like an ostrich with its head in the sands," Niccòlo said.

"Get to Sabato. I will need some clothes." He ran a hand over the hefty beard growth on his chin, surprised that not being able to shave should trigger such an idea. He turned to Niccòlo and watched the light dawn in his eyes. How had he thought his brother inept? Aless felt a sudden bout of affection, then gratitude towards him.

"*Si*," Niccòlo said softly. "Are you certain of this, Aless? Do you truly believe Padre is mad enough to chance seizing Chalmers?"

"Everything points to that end."

"'Twould be perfect if we had wind of the Conte's disreputable plans."

"No one ever claimed life was perfect," Aless grimaced. "Though, I admit, a little more information would not be amiss."

"Do you truly believe Padre has lost his mind, Aless?"

Alessandro considered the question. "*Si*, I do. But I believe it has been years in the making. 'Twas nothing we could have saved him from."

"Will a stigma attach to you, do you suppose, by pretending to be him? After all, your resemblance to him is remarkable. And people..."

"Is there another choice?" he snapped. It was not as if he hadn't thought that very thing. His very future with Essie—Lady Esmeralda—hung in the balance. The irony of the situation struck him with the bark of a painful laugh. "I think not, Niccòlo." It would only be to convince his father's men to stand beside him. Aless, after all, had experience in the leadership of war. 'Twas time to put those skills to better use. Use that would save lives, not take.

"Lady Esmeralda will be proud to call you husband."

Aless winced at the unexpected admiration coloring his brother's tone. "Let's not get carried away." After all, Niccòlo was unaware of Aless's unfortunate slander.

Niccòlo grinned, thoughts apparent on his face. "*Si,*" was all he said. He rose to his feet with a painful scowl. "Do not worry. I shall return."

Chapter 37

ON FURTIVE, QUIET STEPS Niccòlo held a hand to his wounded shoulder and molded himself to the wall. He counted the rosary beads in his head. With each "Hail Mary" he prayed that not only would one fail to discount his presence, they would steer clear of his chosen path to Aless's chambers as well.

His luck almost held out.

"And where might *ton frère* be, my friend?" Joseph Pinetti smirked, his relaxed form blocking the doorframe.

Niccòlo schooled his features but was afraid Pinetti had already seen through his façade. "My brother? Alessandro?" Niccòlo winced. Well, that was convincing.

"Come now, Niccòlo. The admirable Lady Esmeralda is missing and has been for much of the night and day. Word has it that Alessandro was confined in the dungeons but..." Pinetti shrugged. "I daresay he will be married before the week is out."

"If he lives that long," Niccòlo muttered under his breath.

The door behind Pinetti opened throwing Pinetti off balance. Pinetti's startled embarrassment comforted Niccòlo somewhat.

"Come in. Quickly," Sabato demanded. His soft tone did not diminish the fierceness. "I daresay you shall require this." He thrust a great cape into Joseph's arms.

"How—"

"Does it matter?" Joseph uttered. His shrewd gaze on the manservant was prudent, Niccòlo decided. "What do you propose, old man?" Joseph asked him.

Niccòlo answered for him. "Aless plans to masquerade as the Conte."

"Ah, then he took my warnings seriously."

"Take this, but heed it most carefully." Sabato's tone was solemn. He held out a small box covered in dark violet silk, embroidered with delicate yellow rosettes and trailing green leaves. It appeared Orient in nature. Byzantine?

"Your warnings?" Niccòlo frowned. "What is this for?"

"'Tis good of you to offer your services, Monsieur Pinetti," Sabato murmured. "We've not much time, I fear."

"I didn't hear him offer his services," Niccòlo muttered, opening the box. He was terrified it would splinter it into a million pieces with his clumsiness. He gasped at the rich content. A bracelet in the shape of a dragon, emerald eyes shimmering, a tongue lined with rubies, and body covered in a myriad of brilliant diamonds that seemed alive lay upon a bed pf velvet. And worth a small kingdom.

"What services! Where did this come from?" Niccòlo hissed. "What is going on, I ask you?" He failed to control exasperation that finally burst through. These two were seeing something in the atmosphere Niccòlo obviously missed. But there was scarcely time to contemplate the issues.

"Aless will understand its necessity," Joseph said.

"I've gathered other items that may be useful, as well," Sabato said, handing Joseph a worn black cloak and fine black beaver hat lined in taffeta.

Niccòlo started to turn, but Sabato stopped him.

"Don't forget this, my son."

But Joseph reached over quickly and confiscated a pistol Niccòlo had never seen before he realized what was happening. "What the hell is that?" Niccòlo voice sounded strangled.

"A Spanish Breech-Loading pistol," Joseph grinned. He clapped Niccòlo on the back as if he were a small child, sending a sharp pain through his injured shoulder. "Do not worry so. Your brother knows how to shoot."

Niccòlo chose not to respond to that. He rolled his eyes and growled, "Let us be off."

Chapter 38

ESSIE SQUEEZED HER EYES tightly against tears welling up and furious blinking. Had Edric made it back safely? If anything happened to him, she would die. She tried to wriggle her fingers but her efforts made them numb. The way she'd been tossed in a corner, much like a bale of hay, had her thankful for the trousers she'd had the foresight to don.

She made it to a sitting position. She needed her every advantage. A slight scuffling caught her attention. She stilled.

As did her captor.

Something about the scuffed pattern threatened to try her last nerve, slow...methodical. Her belly coiled with tension, head still pounding from the original blow she'd taken.

If she could just loosen these bonds...

ANGER SOARED THROUGH Alessandro's veins, almost blinding. From his vantage point he could make out Essie struggling against bindings that held her wrists. He checked his surroundings, lifted a finger to his lips towards Joseph and Niccòlo. They nodded an acknowledgment.

If he just could signal her somehow. He hated to do it, but he stepped back until she was out of his line of vision. He needed some bold stroke of genius to distract that heathen from her.

He reached for the bracelet Niccòlo held out in an open palm, its delicacy overstated by its weight. Running the tip of his finger over the emerald eyes, pricks of premonition raised the hair on his nape—the diamonds were as cold as ice. But when he touched the rubies, he snatched his hand back nearly dropping it due to fierce heat. He would swear he could see the shimmer rising. He darted a glance at Joseph, whose lips tipped into a sardonic smile.

"Beware of the rubies, my friend," he said softly. "While they offer protection, they are most commonly used in love spells and to increase one's energies of the...uh...more fleshly persuasions."

Aless ignored that bit of sarcasm. "If this fails, and mind, I am *not* speaking of the fleshly persuasions, I will personally strangle you," he snapped.

His nerves were strung so tight he thought he would explode into a million particles. He looked askance toward Niccòlo. "Will I pass for Papa?"

Niccòlo's frown was pronounced. "*Si*, unnervingly so."

"Should you have need of the bracelet, make certain you convey how critical it is she remains still, else we lose our battle on two fronts. Not so much as a blink," Joseph warned. Aless suppressed a groan. Lady Esmeralda not blink?

"Two?" Niccòlo asked.

"The bracelet will deem her invisible to the naked eye and anyone touching her. But if she so much as twitches, we—*she*—becomes vulnerable. Our opponents may then realize the weapon we harbor in this small powerful jewel," Aless said. "What power does that scepter you hold wield?"

"Power?" Joseph glanced down at the staff in his hand and frowned. He appeared to have forgotten the small staff he held. "This thing holds no power. 'Tis only for show. And spearing, cleanly."

Aless swallowed the large lump that suddenly wedged in his throat. Well, that was reassuring. He knelt down, confirming the presence of the knife hidden in his boot. 'Twas there, though the action comforted him little. He checked the pistol at his back Sabato had also conveniently packed for him, praying he had no need of it. That would send the castle into an uproar and have him strung up by his heels before he could utter "God save the Queen."

"The plan is simple, Joseph," Aless said. "You shall swoop in first drawing his attention. That should allow you ample time to do whatever trick it is you do to manipulate him in leading us to the others." He looked hard at his brother. It was time. Time to place his trust in his younger *fratello*. "Once that barbarian is under Joseph's mesmerizing powers, Niccòlo, I'll render Lady Esmeralda invisible and guide her to you. Then you must whisk her to the safety of her family. Joseph and I shall then take care of the Conte."

"Aless—"

He quelled Niccòlo with a glance. "No more. We must act."

Moments later, to Aless's surprise, the pirate fool had not the forethought to hide himself any further than slightly deeper in the corridor where Aless had found Niccòlo. He positioned himself from both the pirate's and Essie's sights.

His prayer now consisted of Niccòlo delivering his future bride safely into the bosom of her family and somehow righting what wrongs his father had up his conniving sleeve. And that meant a clean escape.

With an outrageous bout of dramatics, even for Joseph, his friend swept forward. If Aless had not been so fearful of the outcome, he knew he'd be stifling a grin. As it was, he stood with blade in hand prepared for the worst. This certainly was on par with some of their school day antics, except for the knife of course, though never had so much been at stake.

"What is the meaning of this?" Joseph's stage voice boomed.

"*Dio*—who are you?" Thankfully Joseph had startled the simpleton.

Aless felt his heart in his throat when the man did the unthinkable and charged, not for Joseph, but Essie. Without a second's hesitation Aless let the blade fly from his fingertips. It pierced the villain's neck with a sickening thud.

By the time Essie's gasp escaped, Aless was on his knees beside her, her head cradled in his hands. Her shock was so complete her eyes froze in a wide uncustomary stare—before succumbing to their customary flurry of frenzy, threatening their limited light source.

"Oh my God," he whispered. He wrapped her in his arms. His relief had his knees quavering. He could feel her gulping for air, striving for calm. He planted his face in the crook of her neck, reveled in the faint floral scent he could still detect. "Close your eyes, Darling. Don't look." She nodded against his chest, and with a shaky breath, leaned away. Grasping her by the upper arms, he lifted her to her feet and turned her to the windows. His fingers trembled so badly he could barely loosen the ties on her wrists.

"Aless—" Niccòlo started. The urgency in his tone alerted him to a new danger. Then he heard the reason.

With only a second to spare, the twine dropped away giving Aless seconds to slip the bracelet around Essie's wrist, rendering the two of them unseen. He lifted and turned her into his chest, could feel her lashes fanning the thinness of his shirt. Heat from the bracelet's rubies seeped into his skin, stirring his blood, uncomfortably.

"What goes on here?" Prince Charming demanded.

Aless's panic was nearly as pronounced as Essie's nerves. If the prince found him, he would ne'er be able to stop the Conte—Chalmers Kingdom would indeed fall to the enemy.

"He's dead." Sir Arnald was very astute.

"We found him like this, Sire." *Thank you, Joseph.*

"To whom does this knife belong?" The prince stooped down and jerked the dagger from the villain's throat. Aless held his breath, and edged Lady Esmeralda away from the loose bindings near their feet as Niccòlo gasped at the violence.

If she so much as blinked...

The words reverberated through Aless's head. Her heart pounded against his. If she lifted her head, they were done for. He lowered her feet slowly to the floor willing her belief in him, however blind it warranted. His message was not getting across. So much for visionary connections of love. Her body raged fire against his. He would go mad if his efforts for Chalmers safety all went to naught. Aless could feel his power of will for Lady Esmeralda growing weaker.

He moved his fingers over her lids, felt her breath catch, and before he could convince himself of the monumental mistake he was making, he slid his mouth over hers, let the rubies have their way—in total surrender. The voices surrounding them became a blurred hum, thrumming though his veins.

Her shock quickly turned to a yield that hitched his own breath. Her arms stole about his neck and she molded her body to his as sweet as a gentle rain in spring. He gripped her firmly; hands on either side of her face, and delved his tongue into the warmth of heaven.

ESSIE WAS AWARE OF nothing but the large warm hands clutching her heated cheeks and rapid breath as Alessandro pulled his lips from hers. *He'd put his tongue in her mouth.* The sensation was...was so foreign...so titillating, that her first inclination was to shove him away. But the moment seized her like nothing before. Was this how Cinde felt at the first ball?

Non! It could not have been. This was more intimate, engulfing. She felt almost as if she'd lost her innocence, yet didn't mind in the least. Lord, what would it take to stop Maman from maiming her should she discover such wantonness?

She loved it. Saints in Heaven! She loved *him.*

Was this not same man who'd declared to his father only days before he'd ne'er be bound for life to a woman whose eyes fluttered so furiously, 'twas enough to create an avalanche? The very thought of words coming from such sweet tasting lips made her ill. Did he still cling to that conviction?

Slightly horrified by her acquiescence without even the slightest hint of even the tiniest struggles, Essie drew in a shaky breath and lifted her eyes to his. She must know. To her utter amazement and delight and *relief,* Alessandro's dark eyes were filled with a sense of surprised bemusement.

A soft thrill tripped through her that made her heart sing. Open palms heated her skin through the thin cotton shirt she wore. Voices slowly invaded her senses.

"Where is Aunt Sessie?" Edric cried. "The mean man take-ed her."

Edric? She tried to jerk her head from Alessandro's shoulder but he held her in place. She stilled.

"Take him away," Prince barked. "And get someone in here to clear away the mess."

Essie turned her head in the direction of the guard and promptly regretted it. Dragging her captor through a thick pool of blood, the guard hoisted him over his shoulder leaving no doubt of the man's lifeless fate. She opened her mouth unable to hold back a gasp of horror, but Alessandro gripped her head, forcing her face into his shoulder. Her stomach roiled, her knees buckled. Only the tight hold he had about her waist kept her from collapsing to the ground in an undignified swoon.

Chapter 39

"FIND THEM," PRINCE GROWLED.

Aless stiffened and pulled Essie deeper into his chest anchoring their positions.

"I'll have his head."

The guard moved out of the room with his dead cargo. The stench of blood most prevalent.

"Papa."

Essie started at the tiny voice. Hand on her nape, Aless pressed in warning. She froze. Message heeded, he prayed. Leastways, she could realize Edric was safe.

"Son! Stay back."

Aless remained rigid, not daring a move. The slightest twitch could give them away.

"Where's Aunt Sessie?" Aless could see the child struggling against whoever held him restrained.

"She's not here, Edric. I'm sorry."

"You kill-led the bad man, Papa. I saw him." The little prince pressed his lips together, somewhat reminiscent of his aunt. "If I had a sword I would have run him through."

"I told you to wait for me at the end of the corridor. You disobeyed my direct orders."

Edric sniffed loudly, sounding dangerously close to tears. "But, Aunt Sessie needs me to rescue her." Aless felt the slight tip of a smile deep within his soul.

"Edric, I shall find your Aunt. You shall return to your Maman. She is sure to slay me once she learns of this scenario," Prince muttered.

It seemed forever as Edric rattled on before their voices finally echoed down the vacant hall. Aless was certain Prince Edric had no cares along those lines, regardless. Aless would hate to find himself in Prince Charming's position once Princess Cinderella learned the true events.

He stepped back from Essie though he found he not ready to relinquish his hold. "Are you well, my lady?'

"*Certainement*," she said breathlessly. She kept her eyes averted from the bloodied area of the floor, riveted to the bracelet on her wrist. "What is this?"

"It renders you and anyone touching you, invisible. The effect is not quite stable if you move."

"You mean Prince, Sir Arnald, Niccòlo, Monsieur Pinetti..." her voice trailed.

"*Sì.* No one suspected we were within arm's reach. Come. We must remove ourselves before they return."

"Why would they return?" she asked, eyes still fastened on the jewels, awed marring her pert features. Then she seemed to start to their present situation. "Oh, right. The b-blood..." She moved a hand to her stomach.

"We shall get you to safety before I deal with the Conte and his schemes. I only pray I am not too late."

"You cannot hope to handle him and his band of outlaws on your own?" she gasped. Her gaze narrowed, suddenly focusing on his attire. "Why, they will mistake you for *him* dressed as you are."

"'Tis the idea," he grimaced.

"*Non*," she stated. "I will not allow it."

"*Sì*," he said firmly. "You have no say in the matter." He navigated their way past the disgust on the floor.

"But you shall be outnumbered, and without the protection of the castle," she protested.

"I shall be fine. You, my lady, will do as I say. Your family is very worried for you." He lifted her small form over the last of the bloody streaks through the door. She weighed but a farthing.

Her compressed lips were not reassuring, but she would do what he said, or face the consequences. He set her on her feet but maintained a grip on her wrist, fire from the rubies searing his blood. She spun to face him her other hand fisted at her hip. Anger flashed turning her green eyes into shards of emerald fire. Nary a blink. She opened her mouth to speak. Lash out, more likely. "You—"

Damned if he couldn't resist her one last time. He was lost, he thought, laying his mouth over hers. He drank in her surrender. She was his, utterly and completely. And he planned to show her exactly that once this mess with the Conte and the Prince was resolved.

He lifted his head.

Her breath escaped in rapid short intakes. "You do not play fair, *Signore*."

"Shush," he whispered against her hair. Soft curls tickled his nose. "Go. Let your family know you are well."

Her small hands braced his shoulders. She moved back a step, widening the space between them. Prepared for her argument, he set his jaw. To his surprise, she only considered him a moment longer, a wispy smile upon her lips, before fading from sight. Aless closed his eyes and dropped his hands to his sides. Steadying his breath, he listened to her footsteps fade beyond the corner before he started for the same direction.

He groaned. *Dio.* He'd forgotten to retrieve the damned bracelet.

There was no time to worry for that now. He had the Conte to stop.

THE ARROGANT CUR!

Did he think himself infallible? What if Prince came after him with an army and Alessandro suffered a lapse in memory again? Essie pressed her lips into stubborn line. Whether the man realized it or not, he needed assistance, and she was the only one in the position to offer it.

Once she moved from his sight she leaned against the wall and waited. She stared down at the brilliant piece donning her wrist. There was a distinct trail of heat where the rubies breathed fire around her wrist. A truly odd sensation. It made her feel warm in unspeakable places. How on earth did it render a person invisible? She grinned. Well, it matter naught. *Oui,* whether he chose to accept it or not, Alessandro de Lecce would indeed have her help.

She sucked in air and froze as whispered footsteps paused nearby. Alessandro had stopped and turned his head. With a muttered oath he would unlikely release in her *known* presence, he moved quietly down the corridor. Amazing—she glanced down at the elaborate bracelet! He ne'er even suspected her presence.

She started after him.

Chapter 40

RAGE RACED THROUGH Pasquale's veins like melting snow thawed too quickly down the side of a mountain, creating an incredible burning sensation. His anger was so complete it threatened to drop him to his knees. So his elder son thought to best him from the legacy of which he'd been cheated; deciding to side with their enemy, did he?

He peered cautiously around the corner. Alessandro stood alone, appearing weary, head back and eyes closed. Dressed remarkably similar to him! Truly, did Alessandro believe he could overthrow all his plans, years in the makings? Power was finally days, if not hours, within his grasp.

The intensity of the burn simmering beneath the surface of his son's skin had the air shimmering with movement. A moment later Alessandro stirred into action, all signs of weariness—in the set of his jaw, the gait of his stride—dissipating.

Pasquale shook his head. Well, no sacrifice too great. He truly loved his elder son, 'twas such a waste. He clutched his chest at the sudden pain of the loss he was about to incur. But then pressed his lips together tightly. Such sacrifices had to be made. Alessandro must be stopped before he ruined everything.

Even at the cost of his son's death, Pasquale vowed not to hesitate to instill brutal methods. Honor would be avenged.

Chapter 41

THE TRICK NOW WAS to escape the castle unseen. Keeping a watchful eye, Alessandro set a pace that would do a hungry lion on the prowl proud. According to the Conte, the troops were gathered at the southern most end of the forest wall, just beyond the palace grounds. Aless knew the place well. A place where many picnics were held, and young bucks observing potential mates could be found, spying over the small valley. The young women no doubt considered themselves safe from roving eyes. He, however, knew better.

It unnerved him how brazen his father had chosen to host these meetings so close to the castle. And how was he financing these outrageous endeavors?

Blast! 'Twas the smuggling operation Lady Pricilla and Sir Arnald stumbled upon some five years ago! That must be it.

He felt somewhat ill at what he'd failed to see. So much could have been avoided. Aless pulled himself and shook his head—ridiculous. 'Twas not possible. Yet... *No*! He refused to believe it. But could he afford not to? Was his father the monster behind Lady Pricilla's abduction?

"Dio," he hissed. If his father *was* the villain smuggling weaponry Lady Pricilla and Sir Arnald happened upon, it was safe to conclude that he would stop at nothing to take over Chalmers. That last thought sent him into a dead run.

The nip in the air was brisk. Trees swayed in slight protest, fortunately masking his footsteps. Winter was not long off. Aless slipped through the trees unseen and made his way quietly and efficiently toward a valley surrounded by a copse of trees.

His journey seemed forever before finally reaching the visual perimeter. He gasped at the sight that met him, terrified him rather. Close to a hundred men milled the area with no sign of leadership. Tension permeated the atmosphere. It showed in the gathering of a small group surrounding two shabbily dressed soldiers. They circled, each eyeing the other warily, knives in hand at the ready.

The snap of a twig jerked his attention from the scene before him. Crouching low, Aless scanned the area behind him.

Nothing.

With a steadying inhale, he stood slowly. It was time to take care of the Conte's mess before it turned into full-frontal war. Aless glanced around one last time, hair standing at his nape, and inhaled deeply before taking on the persona of his now-nemesis.

"DEAR GOD," ESSIE GASPED. Someone was about to be killed. So surprised she was at the scene below that she failed to notice Alessandro slip from her view. He appeared again down the hill barking an order.

The disorderly group fell into something akin to a line. Essie watched, fascinated, yet horrified at Alessandro's audacity. He raised his arm in a large sweeping motion. She was not close enough to hear his words, but the effect on the men proved...mesmerizing. 'Twas the only description that came to mind. The group lined up side by side, eyes riveted on Alessandro without so much as a blink. Well, at least from this distance.

She edged forward, compelled by the timbre of his voice. An overwhelming sensation of being enveloped in his arms once more swept through her. It roared through her veins like a feverish plague. She had to get to him before he was harmed.

But then the most amazing sight met her. She froze.

Weapons dropped from their grasps, the clang reverberating through the valley. The whole troop of men fell to their knees, arms crossing their chests in a sign of fealty. He'd done it. She couldn't fathom how, but unless the sight before her was a mirage, they believed him his father.

Essie started down the hill, when movement from the corner of her eye startled her.

"Aless!" she screamed.

THE MOST SICKENING SENSATION Aless would ever have the misfortune to know exploded from the center of his gut. Lady Esmeralda's terrified scream warning him. He spun and dived to the ground in time to avoid the glinted point of his father's sword.

He rolled and swept up another near at hand.

"What have you done?" The Conte growled. His face, twisted in a sneer of mad evil.

"I'm saving your neck, old man." A scarlet flush rushed his face.

Aless wondered if he'd drop in a fit of an apoplexy. He'd never spoken to his father so. He sidestepped another lunge. Barely just, as the blade sliced his upper arm in a blaze of fiery pain. Aless just missed with his own swipe.

"Aless!"

Hell. "Stay back," he hissed at her.

"You...you're bleeding," she choked. Velocity in wind increased. Dust and leaves filled the air.

Moisture tripped the atmosphere where a water spout leaped skyward from a nearby pond.

Sí, he was bleeding, but the fire and pain he felt was not from his arm. Quit blinking, he prayed—'twas the only way to remain invisible.

His father let out a sad laugh. "My regret is true, but, you, my son, are expendable." Coiled and predatory, the bastard spun and snagged Esmeralda by the waist, using her to shield his body.

"I shall kill you," Aless vowed.

"Eh? Straight through this lovely, my son *and heir*? 'Tis too late, either you side with me or die, you know. They will never believe you were not a part of my plans."

"Never!" Aless's voice was husky and steely, his fury complete. The Conte flinched. When he touched Lady Esmeralda, he'd signed his own death warrant.

"I've heard how you speak to her."

"He...he speaks to me a certain way?" she squeaked. As if now was the time for these ruminations. Aless steadied his sword. He dare not swing.

"*Sí*, my dear." The Conte's voice held a humorous note incongruous of the time and place.

"Let her go, Padre." Alessandro's throat constricted. "Surely, you cannot mean harm to the lady."

Maniacal laughter filled the valley. "I care not, son. I am as good as dead if my plans are not seen through." Esmeralda gave a choked cough as the Conte's grip tightened. "Men! Retrieve your weapons," his father commanded.

But they would not, Aless knew. They were well and truly mesmerized. The Conte's dreams of ruling were over.

"In...um...what manner does he...um...speak to me that is different?"

Aless clenched his jaw. She wanted to converse on the specifics now?

"He fights love—"

"Love!" she said sharply. Her eyes narrowed on Aless, and to his dismay, heat crawled up his neck. Nary a blink occurred at this declaration. The wind stilled, the leaves dropped, the water spout pooled into little ripples. She and the Conte faded from sight.

Aless had no problem with Lady Esmeralda learning of his love. *No*, the problem was in the audacity of his father conveying it to her in such a manner. "Men," he called out. "Retrieve your weapons." He prayed this worked.

The throb in his arm palpitated in synchronization with scraping metal.

Chapter 42

WITHOUT WARNING THE MEN snapped to attention. Essie watched, heart in her throat, as they brandished their weapons. Prepared for what, she could not fathom. Dread consumed her. What if they turn on Alessandro? Killed him right before her eyes. She gasped at the very thought.

All around her, words thrummed in the air, undecipherable.

"Where did they go?"

"They were there but a moment past!"

"Lud! Vanished into thin air—"

The grip about her waist tightened, suddenly constricting her breath, forcing her eyes to squeeze tight against the pain. By all the saints, she and the Conte had disappeared. She had to move.

"What are those nitwits talking about, Aless?" The Conte demanded.

Yet, they surrounded Essie and the Conte, moved in closer.

"Call them off, Aless," the Conte growled. "I swear I shall kill her."

Oh, *non*. Essie swallowed. He was going to do it. The Conte was going to kill her. Her nerves could not take it. The wind stirred violently. Dry soil scratched her eyes, yet she could not contain her fear.

"Why did you do it, Padre?" Alessandro's voice carried accusation laced with something akin to fear. Not for her, surely? "You've been smuggling weapons for years, *no*? It was you who ordered Lady Pricilla's abduction, *no*?"

The Conte shook his head, his care unseen. "That was nigh on five years past. What has that to do with now?"

"Y-you?" Essie stammered, aghast. "You almost killed my sister!" Essie was so angry she stomped her kid boot into his instep, startling him. His grip loosened and she jabbed her elbow into his rib at the unexpected opportunity. He doubled over.

Things happened quickly after that. She found herself felled to the ground in an unceremonious heap. She pulled herself to sitting, wincing at wrench in her wrist. Unruly hair blocked her vision, and she shoved it back.

"Alessandro!" Essie scrambled to her feet. The sword he held touched his father's neck, drawing blood.

"How did I miss the signals, Padre?" He sounded angry with himself.

"Alessandro. I beg you, do not kill him." Essie tugged at his arm, but it was as rigid as a solid bar of iron. Unmovable.

"Well?" Alessandro demanded—completely ignoring her.

"You don't understand. They stole our heritage." The Conte's whimpered desperation whistled through his teeth.

"You would endanger young, innocent women? For what? Money? Power?"

"You are an ungrateful son," the Conte hissed.

He gaggled as the sword pressed forward.

"Aless, please..." Essie begged. "You cannot kill your father; your regret will be insurmountable."

"Well?" Alessandro demanded, his eyes never strayed from the tip of his sword. Blood oozed from his father's neck. "She cannot keep me from taking your life, Padre. I'll have the truth, *per favore*."

"*Sí! Sí*, 'twas my right, I tell you. Lady Pricilla only happened in the wrong place at the wrong time. He sneered, obviously recalling the memory. "It was just bad luck that she murdered my best confederate."

Prince strode from the trees, Sir Arnald at his side along with twenty or so guards. "Arrest him. Arrest them both."

Chapter 43

"*EXCUSEZ-MOI!*" ESSIE.

"*Mi scusi!*" Alessandro.

Slightly registering their simultaneous outrage, Essie could not believe her ears. "You cannot arrest him," she yelled. One of the guards jerked her by the arm, casting her bodily from Alessandro.

"*Non.*" She ran forward but the blackguard snagged her by the arm again, this time unrelenting in his grip. She kicked out but he dangled her in the air like a rag doll. "Let me *go*. He did nothing."

A sinking sense of horror clogged her throat as another massive guard twisted Alessandro's arm up behind him at an odd angled hold.

He shot her a look full of silent meaning. In a deep and calm resonating pitch, he said, "Be still, my lady."

The message penetrated, and she stilled. They could only remain invisible if she remained immobile. But what to do about the guard? She lifted her foot slowly. 'Twas easy enough to balance since he seemed compelled in maintaining it for her, and brought her booted foot down hard on his instep. It had worked before, after all.

"Auck," he screeched, setting her free. Essie moved back quickly and stilled. A small twitch of approval touched Alessandro's lips. The sight warmed her inside out.

"Where did she go?" She watched the guard's confusion with a perverse sense of satisfaction.

Prince Charming pressed his mouth into a tight, thin line and narrowed his eyes on Alessandro before scanning the area for any sign of her. Essie held her breath and squeezed her eyes shut—tight. The wind dropped once more.

A twinge of guilt touched Essie, but she would make it up to Cinde later.

"You'll not escape so easily this time round," Arnald told Alessandro.

"Take them away," Prince said.

"We'll see about that," Essie said under her breath, gazing after the retreating group.

Saints in Heav'n, what she'd give for a hot soak. She was hungry too. Essie did not know what plans it would take to spring Alessandro from his cell. They were sure to be much more watchful this time around. But she would see him free and find some way for him to escape the country.

He would need a horse and supplies, but how did one go about acquiring such things? Subterfuge was decidedly difficult, she decided.

Fists at her hips, she watched Prince stride back the way he'd come, leaving Alessandro and the Conte to the massive guards. The Conte's army was rounded up by the future king's guards, yet they did not seem to remain any sort of threat.

Shocking, that.

After a few moments, making certain the way was clear, Essie picked up her heels and darted after them.

"Hey!" she yelped as she was snagged by the waist.

"Well, *sister dear*."

"Your Highness," she squeaked.

Chapter 44

"I'LL NOT DO IT," ESSIE HISSED.

"Oh, *oui*, you shall do it." Cill barked out a laugh. "You are the talk of the kingdom. Besides, there is a certain romantic element in saving his neck from the garret, *non?*"

"Sarcasm is not your forte," she returned.

"*Certainement*, it is." Cill's brows rose, punctuating her outrageous tone. Cinde, however, sat on the bench in the window taking in the scene in utter silence, her face a mask of blank resignation. The needle she held was poised and threaded, ready for the strip of embroidery resting on her lap.

"Your fate is sealed," Cinde said.

Tears filled Essie's eyes. "I shan't do it. You cannot force me."

"*Je suis désolée*, Essie. I fear there is no choice in the matter." Cinde, at least, sounded as pained by the decision as Essie felt. She bent over her sampler and set the needle to work.

"But what of the Coronation Ceremony? Surely, it will interfere..." Essie's voice trailed. The situation loomed over her like a dark thundercloud bursting with drowning capabilities. She raised her eyes heavenward. "*Miséricorde!*" Breath held, she waited, but alas, the heavens refused to accommodate her request for mercy. Not even the tiniest crack in the floor appeared.

"It matters not," Cinde said. Essie's gaze was riveted by Cinde's nimble fingers that suddenly darted through the fabric as if chased by fire. "Would you have Stepmama select your bridegroom? *Non,* 'tis the best resolution for all parties concerned. Besides, my husband has declared it so. There is naught I can do to save you."

Essie cast a desperate glance about, seeking a refuge, an escape...something. *Anything.*

"'Twas inevitable, Essie," Cill said. "You have to marry. And 'tis clear for all to see that you are in love with Alessandro."

"But he is not in love with me." She gasped at the sharp pain gripping her belly. "Don't you see? Now he is to be punished for life? With a wife who possesses the ability to produce an avalanche with an attack of nerves?" Essie spun and wore a relentless path on the carpet. "I'll...I'll accept Maman's selection of a suitable groom." 'Twas the lesser of two evils.

Essie squared her shoulders and looked up in time to see her sisters trading a calculated glint.

Cinde set her embroidery aside, rose from her perch, and placed an arm about Essie's shoulders in an unfruitful effort of comfort. *No* one could comfort her. She'd rather die than be comforted.

"Do not speak so. She might bind you to the Lady Kendra's portly father. Take my word for it. 'Tis all for the best."

Frenzied hysteria choked her. "What of...Joseph? Lord Pinetti? Maman cannot object to *him.* He is a viscount, the son of an English earl." Her voice ended an octave higher.

The door to the chamber crashed open. Maman waltzed through the arch, hand on her massive bosom. "*Non,* the Earl of Macclesfield is the ideal choice. He is of an age to die within years. You will be wealthy beyond our wildest dreams. 'Tis my greatest desire to see you unbearably and blissfully attached to such masculine superiority."

If Essie had not felt so suffocated she would have rolled her eyes as Maman had only to swoon to assert her ambitions any more clearly. At least she seemed to have shifted her ambitions from the demise of Prince and Cinde. "Maman," she said, faintly.

Cinde's eyes took on an unusual hardening at Maman's heartless statement. "Fine, I shall have my husband speak to Joseph Pinetti tonight, Essie, if that is what you truly desire," Cinde said gently.

Essie swallowed the urge to scream, *Of course that is not what I truly desire.* "What do you suppose Monsieur Pinetti would say, Maman? He has not been consulted, I daresay." Cill shook her head, grinning.

Whether she meant to help or not, Essie appreciated Cill's comments. She did not want to marry Monsieur Pinetti or Lord Macclesfield. Ugh, 'twould make her Maman to Lady Kendra. But neither did she desire a match with someone who did not love her and would find her more hindrance than lover. *Lover?*

Essie brought palms up to her flaming cheeks, somehow managing to restrain a groan. Maman trotted over to her, jowls jingling almost comically. Had Essie not been so horrified by her expression she might have been inclined to giggle. Which, ironically, threatened to bubble up in maniacal mirth.

"Do not worry, *ma chère*, I shall speak to the prince myself."

Cill did roll her eyes at that. Essie only felt nauseated.

"'Tis already settled, Stepmama," Cinde said, mildly.

Maman stilled, unnaturally so, eyes glittering. Essie was momentarily stunned by the malice that radiated.

"If...if I could just be granted a moment to speak with him?"

"*Je suis désolée*, Essie. Prince said you were allowed nowhere near his confinement." Cinde strolled back to her seat in the window and picked up her scrap of fabric, dropped her head, and worked her embroidery with a concentration Essie had not witnessed since their cottage days of long ago. Not just concentration, she decided, but a calmness that struck one as...false?

Chapter 45

"I WANT NOTHING MORE," Alessandro growled. He stared out into the gardens from tall floor to ceiling windows, having suffered through Prince Charming's *fatherly* lecture. Ridiculous when they were all of the same age.

How could he tell the prince what his wife's sister overheard him say so recklessly. He turned to the prince. "Sire, if you force her hand in this you cannot imagine the harm."

"Harm? *Harm?* The speculation of her virtue is all over Chalmers." Prince pierced him with a narrowed, pointed look that Alessandro was certain would have had a lesser man dropping to his knees, groveling for forgiveness.

Alessandro willed the heat from his neck and stiffened his spine. 'Twas not as if he had not cherished the idea of her ravishment. Only that the opportunity afforded was not complete enough. Those damned rubies hadn't helped at all.

"What are you trying to say, de Lecce?"

This time he felt the red creep up his neck. He winced. "'Tis unfortunate she overheard a less than flattering comment I had the stupidity to utter in her unseen presence."

"What was that?"

"I would rather not repeat it, Your Highness, if it's all the same to you."

Prince seemed to weigh this statement, then with a reluctant shrug, let it go. Alessandro let out a relieved breath.

"What of your father?"

"I hand him to you on plate covered in gold," Alessandro said.

The prince's lips twitched suspiciously, before he said, "I suppose you mean on a silver platter?"

"Bah. Take him. Do what you will, but I would ask that you consider my brother in your dealings. He had nothing to do with the Conte's demented schemes."

"I know that. He is but a child." Prince scowled.

Alessandro cleared his throat. "That may well be, but I would urge you to keep the sentiment from his more than sensitive ears."

"*Mais oui*, I see your point." He stifled a cough in his hand Alessandro thought sounded more a laugh. "Now, regarding Lady Esmeralda?"

"I have an idea if you would be so willing..." Aless said. 'Twas blessed luck that Prince Charming knew his wife and her sisters so well.

Chapter 46

"LADY ESMERALDA! I BEG of you, are you *trying* to get me annihilated?" Aless fired. "And how did you escape your protectors-by-committee?"

Esmeralda had long since shed her male attire for a stunning gown. Its deep rich hue of blue silk fit her snugly through to the waist. Puffed, capped sleeves left her shoulders and neck bared—and him wanting.

"'Twas quite odd. I was suddenly left to my own devices, and I fear I took advantage. I have an obligation to at least *attempt* saving your neck!" Essie shot back, affronted.

Aless snagged her by the arm and pulled her into his room before someone spotted her. "Save *my* neck?" Truly, she was the most exasperating woman he'd ever happened upon. "Do you have any idea what the prince is capable of, what he has already spared me?"

"Of course, I do, you ninny." Her bottom lip puffed out, hurt that he'd failed to appreciate her well-intentions.

His attention was momentarily stifled by the picture, that lip beckoning to him. A move that would likely see him killed; he shook his head. "Ninny? This should be good," he muttered under his breath.

She stepped to the door and parted it. "Come," she whispered.

The schemes this girl came up with would give him gray hair before his next year of birth. He doubted Prince Charming would be so charming again.

Still, Aless was intrigued and followed her through the door. She stayed close to the walls with a swift pace, skirts whispering softly. In the meantime, he would suffer the view before him. He grinned. *Such a hardship.*

His grin did not last long, however, when she darted down a dark unused corridor, of which the castle seemed to have aplenty, and slipped through a door leading through a small well-tended garden. "Lady Essie, what are you about?"

"Shush," she had the audacity to admonish.

Stalks of heather lined a path through to a hidden gate he would never have known was there. Apprehension nipped at his nape when her gait picked up speed. He had no trouble keeping up, of course. But he did manage to stifle a groan when she headed into the forest. Mindful that most of the area *was* forest. Where could she be leading him?

Ten minutes passed before she slowed her pace. The cautious peer she thrust over her shoulder had him doing the same. "There," she pointed.

"A horse?"

The triumphant smile she bestowed him was lovely, if confusing. "*Mais oui,* for your escape. I've arranged for supplies as well. Enough to carry you to the coast."

"The coast?" He stopped, stunned. "But that is, at the least, a four day trek."

"*Mais oui,*" she agreed. Those adorable lips turned down in a thoughtful frown. "I considered sending you by boat...but that required too many bribes."

"*Bribes?*" His voice *did not* rise by two octaves. He took a deep breath to steady his temper. "Tell me, *per favore*, you did not really issue bribes?"

"You don't have to sound so ungrateful. I went to a lot of trouble—"

"*Trouble.*" His outrage was outweighed tenfold by hers.

"*Ah, je vais aider une personne...pas la peine...c'est pour vous rejetez sans réfléchir à ce cours. J'essaie de vous sauver d'un destin pire que la mort! Ne comprenez-vous pas? Oh Mon Dieu...les hommes. Ils sont aussi lent que les escargots et n'apprécient pas ce que les femmes font pour eux. Vous devriez considérer le sort de votre tête!*"

Alessandro crossed his arms over his chest lest he interrupt something important, waited until she finally appeared winded. "Are you quite finished?"

Eyes glittering, cheeks heightened with her tirade, she glared, pressing her lips together. Yet, he could not resist the display such a fit had revealed.

"I fear I understood not one word you've articulated," he said, mildly.

She translated slowly as if it were Prince Edric she addressed. "I am trying to help you out, but no, *Monsieur*, you throw it back in my face—with no chivalry to speak of." At the onset of each uttered word, her voice picked up in both speed and pitch. "I am trying to save you a fate worse than death. *Mon...Dieu!*"

"Bah. You are slow as a snail..." The iterative narrative seemed to stoke her anger and she began to pace. "Men! They never appreciate the efforts a woman will go. Bah, you should have your head examined." Throwing her arms skyward, she spun in an aggravated circle. "*Tiens, je ne sais meme pas pourquoi je vous parle?*"

He waited until she faced him fully once more before lifting a questioning brow.

"Why am I talking to you?" she informed him, exasperation complete.

He stifled a grin and considered the horse before shifting his gaze back to her. "*Sí, sí*," he said, nodding his head slowly. "Forgive me for not seeing your plan right away. I vow this shall work out perfectly." He let his gaze slide over the indigo silk, form fitted, expensively-tailored gown. A deep sense of satisfaction touched his spine at the heightened color that flooded her cheeks. He rubbed his hands together as the ideal strategy formulated through his mind.

Alessandro grabbed her hand and tugged her after him.

"What are you doing?" she gasped. She stumbled forward but he caught her up before she reached the ground.

"Making our escape. I should never have doubted you for a moment. You've hit upon the perfect solution."

"Our...our escape?" She actually squeaked, eyes fluttered, leaves littering the ground with the onslaught. "P-p-perfect solution?"

He lifted a brow toward her current attire. "Although, you might have dressed a little more appropriately for an escape on horseback. Ah, but as clever as you are, I'm sure you thought to stash the trousers—"

She stopped so suddenly, he thought he wrenched her arm from its socket. "Escape— trousers—"

"We must hurry, they will surely send out a search party once they discover our absence."

"*Non. Non.* You misunderstand, *Signore.*" Her head shook side to side in an adamant denial, threatening the pins that held her flawlessly dressed curls. "The escape is for *you.*"

"*No.* I'll not go without you," he said. Alessandro surprised himself by lowering his shoulder and catching her by the waist. He had to clamp his arm across the backs of her knees to save an unwanted, yet probable, well-placed kick.

"You cannot take me. They shall force you into an unwanted marriage," her voice muffled against his coat. Fists pounded his lower back he deemed not at all that unpleasant. *Sí,* Essie would make a most excellent wife.

"Who said it would be unwanted?" he demanded.

"You did!" She kicked so violently he had to concentrate on his hold lest he drop her.

"'Twas my mistake," he said softly.

A sudden stillness settled over the forest, over her. "What?" Still muffled, but he felt the heat of her breath seep through his clothing.

Alessandro stopped. He set her feet gently to the ground and placed a finger beneath her chin. "'Twas a terrible, *terrible* mistake." He leaned in and touched his lips to her trembling ones. "I was a fool. I find I do not desire a life without the sudden onslaught of breeze. I will not live without you."

"But..."

"No more talk, love. We are to be married."

"*Love?*" Her eyes started to shimmer with a suspicious onset of tears. And she was squeaking again.

"The Prince has the bishop waiting."

"The bishop?" she whimpered, at which point her fluttering eyes sent another shower of leaves to rain over their heads like celebrating confetti.

Sí, 'twas her doing. He smiled, at the surge in wind.

Epilogue

Six months later

"WELL, DARLING." FAUSTINE SLIPPED her arm in the crook of Thomasine's as they made their way to the library where the family gathered for news of Pricilla and Arnald's long awaited child. "All my dreams are soon to be fulfilled. All three girls are happily wed. Prince is now crowned *King* Edric Osmond Thorn VIII. And soon *I* shall have a lovely, most adorable granddaughter."

"You are certain it will be a granddaughter, *ma chère*?" Thomasine smiled. She tilted her head, acknowledging her sister's list of their mutual accomplishments.

Faustine lifted the tattered silver baton she held in her free hand. "'Tis what I most desire." She sighed. Her frothy pink gown glittered, jewels notwithstanding, like the aura of sparkles surrounding her. They meandered, arm in arm, to the windows.

"Her labor is going well?" Thomasine asked.

"*Mais oui*, as we speak. I can scarcely wait for the results."

"She does appear to be a sturdy advocate."

Faustine grinned, obviously pleased with that statement. "I vow this shall be the first of many."

Thomasine, while not wanting to burst her sister's bubble of pleasure, felt inclined to say, "I would not be so sure, my dear."

"It matters naught, regardless." Faustine wrinkled her dainty nose. "Lady Esmeralda wasted no time, *non*?"

"She was quite determined her sisters not outdo her." Thomasine agreed. She smiled again but lowered her tone as they crossed through a perfectly timed opened door. "Such a shame about their Maman, however."

"Isn't it," Faustine agreed, softly, if somewhat sardonically.

Thomasine lifted a brow at the sadly mended apparatus in her sister's grip. "I'm sure you had naught to do with her untimely mishap? Slipping on water in the corridor? My servants would ne'er allow anything so blatantly obvious."

"Bah! How could you suggest such a thing? Is it my fault she cannot see past her double chins to the floor beneath her? How is she faring, by the bye?"

"Unfortunately, she shall live to rue our happy lives. Though, I must admit relief for Pricilla in this time of need. Thankfully Cinderella has finally seen fit in banishing Lady Roche to the Crofter's Cottage at least to keep her out of harm's way. I still think that girl is much too tender-hearted."

"Do you suppose Lady Roche knew about the Conte de Lecce all along?"

"I daresay that would have complimented her with too much intelligence."

Faustine giggled. "*Mais oui.* I suppose you are right. 'Tis the reason she could not be charged with conspiracy."

"I still harbor nightmares over how close that man insinuated himself within our family." A slight shudder rippled Thomasine.

Faustine hugged her tightly. "But all is well. For the new Conte de Lecce, Alessandro, has vowed his fealty to the Sovereignty. It matters naught to him

242

whether he is of Italian or Spanish nobility. And his Knighthood makes for an excellent match for our dear Esmeralda. Why, I've hardly seen her eyes flutter at all."

"True. 'Tis a shame it will never disappear completely."

"No matter, my dear." Faustine patted her hand like a small child. "She has discovered the secret. That she is the only one who controls that of her own desires, destiny and the like."

"Grandmère, what is taking so long?" Prince Edric stood before Thomasine with both hands fisted at his hips, a frown marring his brow. "I should like to show Auntie Cilla a picture I have painted of her new baby boy."

Thomasine was hard press suppressing a quick laugh at Faustine's offended sniff. "'Tis a girl, I regret to inform you, Edric."

A stubborn scowl touched Edric's expression. He opened his mouth to protest, but the library door crash back. Faustine gaped at her only son, who stood paralyzed beneath the arch. Thomasine filed away the image of her sister's expression for later use.

"I have a *son,*" he boomed.

"Dear heav'n, I am a grandmère. Did you hear that, Thomasine? I am a *grandmère.*" Her joy brought tears to Thomasine's eyes.

Then a most unusual thing happened. The baton within Faustine's grip crumbled into a pile of crystallized powder at their feet. Thomasine's gaze riveted to the little mound.

Esmeralda stepped forward. "What is this?"

Fascinated, Thomasine stilled as Esmeralda leaned down and touched the shiny pile. Thomasine glanced about but no one else seemed to notice anything odd.

The silver mass morphed into a new and shiny scepter that radiated gold shimmers. Esmeralda lifted a surprise gaze to Thomasine then shifted to one of wisdom.

And Thomasine realized in that one moment—

Some fortunate child would become the beneficiary of a different Fairy Godmother's newfound powers through that of the Countess Esmeralda de Lecce.

Books by
Kae Elle Wheeler

The Wronged Princess – book i
The Unlikely Heroine – book ii
The Surprising Enchantress – book iii

The Price of Scorn – book iv, The Evil Stepmother

Books by Kathy L Wheeler
Blooming Series
Quotable
Maybe It's You
Lies That Bind

Scrimshaw Doll Tales (The Wild Rose Press)
The Color of Betrayal
The English Lily (Kae Elle Wheeler)

Martini Club 4 Series
Reckless – Kathy L Wheeler

The Mapmaker's Wife
(To Love a Spy Boxed Set)

About the Author

Kathy L Wheeler/Kae Elle Wheeler graduated from the University of Central Oklahoma with a BA in Management Information Systems and a minor in Vocal Music.

She loves the NFL, NBA, musical theaters, travel, reading, writing and karaoke. She's a member of several RWA chapters, including the Oklahoma Outlaws, the Dallas Area Roamance Authors, and The Beau Monde.

Kathy lives with her musically talented husband in Edmond, Oklahoma, has one grown daughter (who is now a mom, herself) and one bossy cat!

http://kathylwheeler.com
http://facebook.com/kathylwheeler
@kathylwheeler

Made in the USA
Charleston, SC
28 April 2015